The KELPIES'S PEARLS

Molly Hunter

Illustrated by Charles Keeping

CANONGATE KELPIES

First published 1964 by Blackie
First published in Kelpies 1993

Copyright © Molly Hunter McIlwraith 1964
Cover illustration by Vanessa Card

British Library Cataloguing-in-Publication Data
A catalogue record for this book is available
on request from the British Library.

ISBN 0 86241 443 1

Printed and bound in Denmark by Nørhaven A/S

CANONGATE PRESS, 14 FREDERICK STREET,
EDINBURGH EH2 2HB

TO MY GOOD FRIEND
THYRA PEARSON
OF ABRIACHAN

Contents

CHAPTER I

The Kelpie

THE story of how Morag MacLeod came to be called a witch is a queer one and not at all the sort of thing you would expect to happen nowadays. It was never proved, mind you, that she *was* a witch. Nobody has decided that to this day – but that is because they did not know about the kelpie's pearls. And it was the pearls, of course, that were the real cause of all the trouble.

To begin at the beginning however, this Morag MacLeod was an old woman that lived alone in a little house high up on the wild stretch of mountain country rising from the north bank of Loch Ness in the Scottish Highlands. Little farms called 'crofts' are dotted here and there on this high land, and there are a lot of little streams – or 'burns' as the Highlanders call them – running down through the heather. It is from these burns and the little graceful roe deer that come to drink at them that the place gets its name, for in the Gaelic – which is the old language of the Highlands – it is called Abriachan, and this means 'the place where the deer come down to the water'.

One of these burns ran past Morag's house and gathered in a deep pool beside it. The pool had a high bank crowned with bracken and heather on the side farthest away from her house but the bank on the near side was shallow which made it easy for her to draw water from the pool. This she did every evening, and after she had filled her bucket she liked to sit by the pool for a while and look down on the dark blue waters of Loch Ness in the valley below.

It happened then that while she was sitting like this by the pool one fine spring evening she heard a voice calling,

'Old woman! Old woman!'

Morag gave a start and looked all round but there was no one to be seen.

'I am getting old, surely,' she said. 'I am beginning to imagine things!'

'You are old right enough,' said the voice, 'but you did not imagine *me*. I am *here*, do you not see?'

It seemed to Morag that the voice came from behind a big boulder at the edge of the burn. She got to her feet and looked round the other side of it, and there was a little old man as shrunken and shrivelled as a nut and all dripping wet.

'Well!' she said in amazement. 'Who are you at all?'

'I am a kelpie, mistress,' the little man snapped as cross as two sticks, and Morag began to laugh.

'Well,' she said when she had done laughing, 'so it's a kelpie that's in it! To think I should have lived to be seventy-two before I see a kelpie!' And she began to laugh again.

'Och, you have bad manners, old woman!' shouted

the kelpie. 'There is no need to laugh just because you see a kelpie!'

'Bad manners, is it!' Morag said sharply. 'Then your manners will not mend mine if you talk so disrespectfully to your elders.'

'You will be old before you are older than me,' shouted he, 'for I have lived in this burn for two hundred years!'

Morag was surprised at this, as well she might be, but she saw no reason to doubt what he said, and feeling sorry that she had offended him she said politely,

'Ah well, let us not quarrel over a hundred years or so. But I would like you to know that my name is Mistress Morag MacLeod.'

'A good name,' said the kelpie, polite in his turn. 'And now, Mistress Morag, if you will look down here you will see that my foot is caught between two stones. I have not the strength to free it – not in the shape I am in at the moment, anyway.'

He gave a Morag a cunning look when he said this but she was looking at the place where his foot was caught and she did not see the expression on his face. She worked the stone away from his foot and the kelpie sat rubbing the ache the pressure of the stone had left in it.

'I am very grateful to you, Mistress Morag,' he said. 'I will give you some pearls from the big river to reward you.'

Morag smiled at him. 'I would be a queer one to want a reward for an act of human kindness,' said she, 'and besides, I am an old, withered woman. What would I be doing with pearls?'

'You could sell them in the big town,' suggested the kelpie. 'They would be very fine pearls.'

'And what would I be doing with the money?' Morag asked. 'I have no need of money, kelpie, for I

have a flock of white hens that are very good layers, and once a week when the bus goes down the hill from Abriachan to Inverness I leave eggs and the vegetables I grow in my garden at the roadside for the driver to pick up and deliver to the grocer in the town. The grocer sends me back tea and other things that I cannot grow on my croft and that takes care of all my needs.'

'It is not the way of our people to be beholden to a human,' the kelpie said sullenly. 'Surely there is something I could give you?'

'There is nothing I lack,' Morag told him, 'except that sometimes I am lonely for someone to talk to that can remember the days when I was young. But the thought was kind, and I thank you for it.'

She bent to pick up her pail and the kelpie watched her with a strange expression on his face.

'Are you not afraid of me, Mistress Morag?' he asked. 'Do you not know that people say the kelpie will drag a mortal down to his home in the deeps of the water? Have you never heard how the kelpie roams in the shape of a big, black horse and whoever mounts that horse to cross a river will be carried down, as well, to the bottom of the river?'

'I know all these things,' said Morag calmly, 'but I am not afraid, kelpie, for I do not think it is in your mind to harm me.'

She wished him good night and walked back to the house with her brimming pail. 'Well, now I have seen a kelpie,' she said to herself as she walked, and she wondered if she should tell Alasdair the Trapper about it the next time he stopped by with a brace of rabbits for her. But Alasdair was a modern man that did not believe such nonsense as kelpies and so she decided to wait and see if the kelpie would come back again before she said anything to anyone.

The next evening then, she went down to the pool as usual to draw water, and sure enough the kelpie was there. He was sitting on a stone at the edge of the water and as Morag drew close he wished her good evening and went on with his game of throwing stones into the water with a sideways twist of his hand so that they bounced off the surface two or three times before they

13

sank. Morag filled her pail; then she straightened up and watched him for a while. The kelpie went on throwing and at last she said,

'That was a game I played often at this pool when I was a little girl.'

'See can you still skiff a stone then,' said the kelpie, handing her one.

Morag turned it over in her hand and exclaimed, 'But kelpie, this is a pearl!'

'Och, there is nothing to that,' said he airily. 'There are always pearls to be found in the big river.'

'But it is too round and light to be a skiffer,' Morag objected. 'We used always to play with flat stones that were heavier than this.'

'Round or flat, heavy or light, if I say it will make a skiffer it will make a skiffer,' the kelpie said irritably. 'Now throw if you want to throw.'

So Morag threw the pearl and to her delight it bounced off the surface of the pool three times before it sank. 'I'll take you on at a game, kelpie,' she cried. 'I still have the cunning in my hand for it.'

'Done!' cried the kelpie, getting ready to throw. And so their game began and it lasted as long as the kelpie had pearls to throw. Morag had never enjoyed a game of skiffers so much in her life even though the pearls *were* a bit light to throw. However, they bounced off the water as well as any flat stones had ever done and she wondered to herself whether this had something to do with the kelpie's claim that anything he said would make a skiffer would make a skiffer.

At the end of the game they sat down and talked and Morag told the kelpie more about her croft. 'My house is very old,' she said, 'for it was built in my great-grandfather's time, but it is still very snug and strong for all its great age. The walls are of clay and straw mixed together and the roof is of pine-boughs thatched with heather, and on either side of my front door I have a bush of small white roses that smell as sweet as anything under heaven. I have a little garden too, where I grow herbs and beyond this is the field where I grow oats, and hay for winter feeding for my cow. Then there are my sheep which give me wool for carding and spinning, and every so often Alasdair the Trapper calls in on me with a brace of rabbits for the pot. So you see, kelpie, I lack for nothing.'

'I still do not like to be under a debt to you,' the kelpie said.

He spoke so sourly that Morag could see he was still set on giving her some of his pearls. She went back to the house feeling rather troubled about this and wondering what she should do, but the next morning something happened that put the problem of the kelpie and his pearls out of her mind for the time being.

CHAPTER 2

King Solomon's Ring

IT was a Saturday, the next day, and when Morag came out of her house early that morning she was surprised to see a boy sitting on the bank where she and the kelpie had been the night before. No one ever came near her house as a rule apart from Alasdair the Trapper, and so curiosity made her go down and speak to the boy.

He would be somewhere between ten and eleven years old, she judged, but for all that it was Saturday and no school to go to he had a face as long as a fiddle on him. It was not his miserable face that made her stare, however, it was the polecat ferret that lay curled like a white fur round his neck and the fledgeling blackbird that perched on his head. She looked at him for a good minute and he looked at her and so did the bird and the ferret, and then Morag asked,

'And what have you the long face for – you that is lucky enough to have King Solomon's ring?'

'I have no ring,' he said, looking down puzzled at his bare, dirty fingers.

Morag laughed. 'It is not a real ring,' she explained. 'It is just a manner of speaking. Have you never heard it before?'

'No, I never have,' said the boy, and so Morag sat down beside him on the bank and told him how King

Solomon in the Bible had such a power to draw wild creatures to him that people said he had a magic ring that showed him how to speak their language.

'But that was only a tale made up by ignorant people,' she said. 'It was no magic he had but only the gift of understanding that comes to those with the patience and kindness to learn the ways of wild creatures.'

She looked at the fierce red eyes of the polecat ferret glinting like splinters of cold hard ruby and she added, 'And that is why I am thinking you have the gift King Solomon had.'

'The Woman does not see it that way,' said the boy. He bent his head and gave such a sniff that the blackbird nearly lost its balance, and in no time at all after that, Morag had the whole sad story out of him.

His name was Torquil MacVinish, he told her, and he lived with the Woman on a croft at the foot of the hill where the Abriachan road joins the main road to Inverness. The Woman was a distant relative who had taken him to live with her after his parents died and though she was kind enough to him in her own way she could not abide his animals.

'She told me to take them out and drown them in the loch,' he said, looking at Morag with all the woe of the world in his eyes, 'but I can't do it, mistress – it would be murder! I *can't* do it!'

'And no more you shall,' Morag said indignantly. 'The very idea! Listen, boy, there is a shed at the back of my house where they can stay and no one a

17

penny the wiser. And you can come up every day after school to feed them.'

'I have a lot more than these two,' Torquil said doubtfully.

'Well, it is quite a big shed,' she told him, and so it was all arranged between them.

Torquil spent the rest of the day bringing his animals up the hill and Morag learned their names as she helped to settle them in the shed. The polecat ferret was Polar from his white fur and his back humped like a polar bear's and the blackbird was Dondo which is the little name for Donald. The big white Angora rabbit with fur as soft and pale as moonlight was called Luna. The voles and hamsters were Sugar, Spice and Candy according to their colours, and the lame young pigeon with the sad expression that pigeons have was Sad Sam. Last of all was the moor-hen called Moses, and you can guess how it got *that* name!

It was wearing well on to evening before it was all done and Morag was thinking that it was just about time for her to go down to the pool. However, there was just time for a cup of tea first and so she asked Torquil into the house where they both sat down to tea with scones spread with butter and royal crowdie, which is a kind of cheese made with sour milk and so called because it is tasty enough for royalty to eat – which indeed they probably do.

Torquil was still looking a bit down in the mouth and so, to amuse him while he ate, she told him about the kelpie and his pearls.

'There is no such thing as a kelpie,' Torquil said immediately, and then in the next breath as Morag rose to get her pail to draw water from the pool he asked, 'Can I come down to the pool with you to see him?'

'You have just said there is no such thing as a kelpie,' Morag pointed out reasonably.

'No more there is,' Torquil said, 'but *if* there is, I should dearly like to see one.'

Morag smiled a little at this. 'I do not know if he will come back again,' she said, 'and in any case it would not be a mannerly thing to do to go there just to stare at him.'

'I could hide in the bracken above the pool,' Torquil said. 'I will not disturb him, mistress, I promise you.'

Morag laughed outright this time. 'Very well, you may come,' she agreed. 'But keep well hidden.'

'I'll go and hide now,' Torquil said, and off he ran. Morag waited for a few minutes to make sure that he had plenty of time to settle down in the bracken and then she took her pail and followed him down to the pool.

The kelpie was sitting by the pool as she had hoped, for Torquil's sake, that he would be. He did not seem to be in the mood to talk, however, neither did he offer to start a game of skiffers. He kept looking uneasily around till at last Morag asked what was troubling him.

'There was one of your own kind, a boy, came past a few minutes ago,' he said angrily, 'and I do not like human-kind near my pool.'

'You do not seem to mind me,' Morag pointed out

and the kelpie said, 'Ach, you! Why would I mind you when you have been drawing water from my pool all these years? Anyway, you are quite sensible for one of your kind.'

'But would you not be friendly to another if he came in a friendly fashion?' Morag asked, raising her voice enough to be sure that Torquil heard her in his hiding-place in the bracken above the pool.

'Never!' the kelpie shouted. 'There will always be war between us and human-kind!'

He looked so angry that Morag said no more on the subject, and the next day when Torquil came up to her house to feed his animals she warned him seriously of the danger of crossing the kelpie's wishes.

'You heard what he said, Torquil,' she told him, 'so do not be taking risks. He is not a being of our world, you understand, so that he has no soul. And it is a dangerous thing for one as young as yourself to tangle with a creature that has no soul.'

'But what about yourself?' Torquil asked. 'Will the kelpie not harm you?'

Morag shook her head. 'Come here and I will show you something,' she said, and she took Torquil into her bedroom and showed him a painting that hung on the wall. It was a picture of herself painted by a travelling artist when she was a young girl and it showed her in a white dress with long, golden hair streaming down her back.

'I would not have stopped to speak with the kelpie when I looked like that,' she told Torquil, 'for it is the young and the strong and the beautiful that the creatures of the other world seek to capture and bind to their will. Now I am old and weak and withered and the kelpie is old too so that we have things to talk about that only the two of us can remember, and I think that pleases him. He will not harm me.'

'Very well, then, I am content to have seen him and I will not come near the pool again,' Torquil agreed.

He was a boy that had been trained to the habit of obedience, you understand, and besides, his curiosity about the kelpie was satisfied for the time being. Moreover, the Woman had been so pleased to get rid of his animals that she had asked no questions on what had become of them, and so Torquil thought to himself that if he kept his visits to Morag's house a secret all would be well with him. He put the matter of the kelpie to the back of his mind, accordingly, and never spoke of it or of Morag to anyone.

Morag herself had no chance to mention it to Alasdair the Trapper as she had thought of doing since he was away from the hill that year, part of the time in jail for poaching and part of the time working as a ghillie on a big estate.

The result of this was that for a long time – until the following spring, in fact – no one except the two of them knew anything about the kelpie and during that time everything did indeed go well with them. Morag quickly won the trust of Torquil's animals so that they became as tame with her as they were with himself. And at last she had someone to talk to who could remember the days of her youth, for the kelpie continued to appear every evening at the pool.

As for Torquil, he had never been happier. Every day after school he stole out of the Woman's house and climbed the hill to feed his animals, and for him it was like climbing up to a secret world and going through the door of a dream. Everything up there was so quiet and peaceful after the roar of the traffic passing the Woman's house and the sound of her scolding voice in his ears. There was nothing to be heard there but the brown burns purling over the stones and the peewits calling the lost, sad cry of their kind: nothing to be seen but purple heather and golden bracken, with maybe a pair of hunting buzzards wheeling on big slow wings in a sky as deep blue as the loch below. And always, in the spring and the summer, little brown specks of larks pouring song like golden rain down from the highest point in the sky.

As soon as he had attended to his animals he would go into the house where Morag was waiting for him with tea and scones spread with butter and royal crowdie, and there, with the warmth of a good peat-fire on their faces and the crowdie sharp and tasty on their tongues, the two of them would sit and talk. And this both he and Morag enjoyed best of all.

Torquil talked mostly about animals and Morag was astonished to learn how much he knew about them. He could tell where to find the nest or lair of every kind of bird and animal on the hill-side and had even tracked a wild-cat to its lair high up among some rocks. He

knew a lot about the creatures of legend as well, such as the Phoenix and Pegasus and the Minotaur. Morag had never heard of these before and she was very interested in them, but one day when Torquil was telling her about the Centaur – the creature that was supposed to be half-man, half-horse – she exclaimed,

'But that is just like the Urisk!'

This was something that Torquil had never heard about and so Morag told him about the Urisk which is a creature of Highland legend, only it is half-man, half-goat.

'The Urisk is a surly creature,' she explained, 'but

he is very faithful and loyal in spite of that, and mostly he is servant to the fairy people.'

Torquil looked down his nose a bit at this, boys not being much given to talk about fairies, but Morag said seriously, 'Oh, the fairies were not the little wee folk you read about in story-books nowadays, Torquil. They were a small people all right, but not all that much smaller than other people, and there was a time when the folk of the Highlands went in fear of them and their strange powers. And not only the Highlanders, I may tell you. "Banshee", you know is only the English spelling of the Gaelic word "bean-sidh" – the fairy woman that can be heard lamenting for souls that are about to leave the earth.'

Torquil was not believing all this entirely, of course, but after having been proved wrong about the kelpie he thought there might be a great deal of truth in it some-where. And so he went on questioning Morag until she had told him many a strange tale of urisks and fairies and peerie-men, brownies, gruagachs and kelpies and all the other creatures of Highland lore.

'And were the fairies real people then?' he asked her once, but Morag only laughed and said, 'Who can tell? They all lived so long ago that no one can tell what is fact and what is fancy now in all the stories about them.'

Now this was all very well sitting by a bright fire of peats drinking tea and eating scones, but going back down the hill road in the winter months when it was almost dark Torquil would glance fearfully at the great grey shapes of rocks that jutted out of the hillside and fancy he saw a urisk glowering at him from behind the bare stone, and in the sound of the night-wind he sometimes thought he could hear the wild, lost voice of the banshee calling. He told Morag about this, and it was then that she fashioned for him a little cross from the wood of the rowan tree that grew beside the burn.

As she made the cross she told him of how the white berries of the little rowan tree that grew at the foot of Our Lord's cross became red with His blood so that ever after the berries of the rowan tree have been red and its wood has had a sacred power to preserve people from harm.

'So you see, no ill can befall you if you carry this,' she said as she gave the cross to him. And every night after that Torquil ran down the hill with his fingers touching the cross in his pocket and his heart light with the knowledge that he was safe from all harm.

When he had gone, Morag would go down to the pool to meet the kelpie and very often when they got tired of talking they had a game of skiffers, for the kelpie always seemed to have a supply of pearls on him. Morag sometimes thought to herself that there must be a small fortune in pearls in the pool as a result of their games but since she was not interested in money the idea never bothered her. To please the kelpie, however, she did at last accept the pearl necklace he had made for her.

'It suits you fine,' he told her with a glint of triumph in his strange old eyes when she put it on for the first time. 'You look real bonny with them on, mistress.'

The kelpie was speaking no more than the truth when he said this, for flax-white hair is fine with pearls and so are rowan-red cheeks and blue eyes with a pleasant sparkle of good nature in them. Morag had all these and a good black dress to wear with the pearls as well, and though she laughed at the kelpie for a flatterer she could still see in her mirror the bonny picture she made when she wore them.

She grew to like the necklace so much that soon, instead of wearing it just to please the kelpie when she went down to draw water from the pool, she took to wearing it in the afternoons as well. And that was how Alasdair the Trapper came to learn about the kelpie's pearls when he returned to the hill in the following spring.

CHAPTER 3

Alasdair the Trapper

IT was early in the afternoon before Torquil came up to feed his animals that the Trapper called in on Morag one day, and, bad character as he was, she was quite pleased to see him for he always brought news of any doings on the hill.

'It's yourself then, Alasdair,' she said. 'Come away into the house now, and I will put the kettle on the fire while you tell me all the news.'

Alasdair put his string of rabbits down outside the house and came inside to the fire, and the first thing he noticed was the string of pearls gleaming white against Morag's black dress.

'Now where would a *cailleach*, an old woman, like Morag be getting these?' he asked himself but to Morag he said, 'Och, there is not much doing in the way of news just now, mistress – not unless you count that fine string of beads you are wearing.'

'Beads!' Morag cried. 'These are pearls, Alasdair man!'

'Yes, yes indeed,' said Alasdair slyly. 'I can see that now. But how did you come by such a fine string of pearls, mistress?'

Morag poured out the tea. 'You will not be believing me, Alasdair,' she said as she handed him a cup, 'but I am telling you the truth. I had them from a kelpie that has lived in the burn for two hundred years.'

'This is a sly old one,' Alasdair thought angrily. 'She is for trying to make a fool out of me!' And trying to keep the anger out of his voice he said,

'Now, now, Mistress MacLeod, you know I am a modern man and do not believe such nonsense as kelpies.'

No more he did of course, but in spite of that he listened with his mouth open like a landed trout as Morag told him how she had come to know the kelpie and how they had played skiffers with pearls night after night beside the pool.

'It is a great story indeed,' he said at last, 'and if you are not telling it just to make a joke of me, the bottom of that pool must be covered with pearls.'

'Aye so,' said Morag with a twinkle in her eye, 'but they are a bit light for skiffers.'

'*Skiffers!*' exploded the Trapper. 'I am not thinking of any game, mistress. I am thinking how to get those pearls up from the bottom of the pool.'

'But Alasdair man,' said Morag with her eyes twinkling more than ever, 'it was the kelpie that put the pearls there, and if there is no kelpie then there cannot be any pearls. And you are a modern man that does not believe such nonsense as kelpies!'

Now this brought Alasdair up short, feeling more than a little foolish. Then his eye caught the white gleam of the pearls against Morag's dress and he fell to wondering if there *could* be such a thing as a kelpie, for surely there was no living soul could have given an old woman like her such a present. There was only one thing he was sure of. If there were pearls at the bottom of the pool they would be in his game-bag before sundown or his name was not Alasdair the Trapper!

When he had made up his mind on this he said to Morag, 'Well mistress, you are old enough to be my grandmother and goodness knows you have seen many a thing in your long life, and so it is maybe true that you have seen a kelpie. And if that is so, it is maybe true as well that the bottom of the pool is covered with pearls.'

This made Morag wonder what was coming next and she was not left long in doubt for the Trapper went on,

'Now *you* do not seem to set much store by them, and even if the kelpie does – well, he has the next two hundred years to spend in gathering a new lot to throw away!'

He got to his feet very well pleased with his joke, and much as Morag tried to warn him that it was a wicked and dangerous thing to try to steal the kelpie's pearls, he would not listen to a word.

'Somebody might as well have the pearls,' he said, 'and there is nothing a kelpie can do against a modern man like myself.'

He went out quickly before she could say another word and collected his gear. Then he went boldly down to the pool and peered into the water.

There was nothing to be seen – not even the bottom of the pool, let alone any pearls, for the wind was skirling round the shoulder of the hill and ruffling the surface of the water, and the Trapper straightened up wondering what he could do to find out if the pearls were there.

His eye lighted on the little canvas bag he had thrown down on the bank beside his rabbits. Quickly he tipped out the wire, string, pliers and other odds and ends in it, ran a piece of wire through the hem at the top so that the mouth of the bag was held open, and bound the two ends of the wire firmly to a stout stick he got from a bush growing on the bank.

'Now,' said he, 'I can drag the pool.' And with that, he plunged the bag into the water.

But the bag was too light to sink and after he had made one or two attempts to push it down into the water Alasdair pulled it out again and dropped a stone inside it. The bag sank straight down with the weight of the stone in it the next time he put it in the water, and he began to drag it over the bottom of the pool. Back and forward he swept it and the bag began to feel heavy. He tried to draw it to the surface but it seemed to have caught on something at the bottom of the pool, for no matter how he pulled and twisted at the stick the bag stayed at the bottom.

Alasdair struggled on with it, panting and straining. It jerked to the surface at last, but so suddenly that it took him completely by surprise. He had just time to catch a glimpse of it when the stick was snatched from his grasp, and bag, stick and all went plunging back to the bottom of the pool.

'I doubt the kelpie is working against you, Alasdair,' said Morag's voice at his elbow.

Alasdair whirled round to her. 'Did you see yon?' he demanded. 'That bag was full! It was full to the brim with pearls!' And sitting down on the bank he began tugging off his boots.

'You're never going into the pool!' cried Morag.

'I am that,' said Alasdair, throwing off his jacket. And paying no attention to Morag crying to him not to be foolish and tempt the kelpie, he stepped into the water.

The icy chill of it gripped his knees like an iron band, and for a second or two Alasdair hesitated. Supposing he got a soaking in that cold water for nothing? But no, he had seen the pearls with his own two eyes! Supposing the kelpie caught him? Alasdair shook that thought away.

'I am six foot three in my socks,' he muttered, 'and I am strong and hardy. Anyway, I am a modern man and I do not believe in kelpies.' And he took a deep breath and plunged to the bottom.

Morag watched from the bank, holding her breath as he disappeared. 'If I count to ten and nothing happens, he is safe,' she thought, but she had only reached five when there was a flurry at the bottom of the pool and the surface of the water began to boil white. The next instant Alasdair's head broke through the foam, and beside him the head and shoulders of a great black horse.

'The kelpie!' Morag gasped.

The black horse reared upwards, nostrils flaring red, its sharp hooves striking out at Alasdair's head.

'Look out! Look out, Alasdair!' Morag shrieked.

The kelpie screamed with rage and its hooves plunged down. The Trapper gave a terrified shout and threw himself sideways, clutching at the kelpie's mane to try to force its head away from him. It reared again, swinging its head round and lifting him half out of the water as it tried to reach him with snapping teeth.

Morag ran down the bank shouting wildly to the kelpie to let Alasdair go, but the great horse was too mad with rage to heed her.

'Save me, mistress, save me!' roared Alasdair, dodging and twisting about like a demented eel. But what could an old woman do against the strength of the kelpie that a young man could not?

Morag stood there wringing her hands in the greatest distress, and then suddenly something flashed into her mind. It was a thing she had learned long ago as a little girl from her grandmother – a woman that everyone at Abriachan used to swear was a witch – and the thing she remembered was the spell for binding a kelpie to her will.

She snatched up a piece of string Alasdair had left lying on the bank, broke two twigs off the rowan-tree growing at the edge of the water, and with a couple of quick twists of her fingers bound the twigs together in the shape of a cross. Then she raised the hand with the cross in it above her head and called out at the top of her voice the words her grandmother had taught her.

> 'In Christus name I conjure thee,
> Still as water shalt thou be.
> By this cross within my hand,
> Weak as water shalt thou stand!'

The kelpie was caught with its hooves in mid-air plunging down to strike once more at the Trapper's

head. It froze there at the sound of Morag's voice like a carved black statue of a horse, and when she had finished speaking it dropped its hooves to the water and stood with its head hanging, shivering and soundless while the water streamed off its great black body.

'Come quickly, Alasdair,' Morag called quietly, and the terrified man scrambled out on to the bank. When he got there he did not stop to put on his shoes or his jacket or even to thank Morag for saving him. He just bundled everything together without a word and made off down the hill as fast as his long legs would carry him.

'Ah well,' thought Morag, laughing a little as she watched him go, 'there is punishment enough for a modern man that does not believe such nonsense as kelpies.'

She turned back to speak to the kelpie but he was gone. There was nothing to show that he had ever been there but a white swirl of foam on the surface of the pool and Morag walked back to her house thinking, with a great sadness at her heart, that she would probably never see him again.

'I have seen the last of the kelpie,' were her first words to Torquil that afternoon, and she told him how Alasdair had tried to get the kelpie's pearls. Torquil was quiet for a moment after she had finished; then he said,

'Your grandmother must have been a queer one, surely, to have known how to get the better of a kelpie.'

'Maybe aye, maybe no,' said Morag, and that was all she said though she was not too well pleased at this description of her grandmother. However, she had no intention of telling Torquil that the old woman had been a witch. Witches in story-books, after all, are quite a different matter from real witches and real witchcraft, which are serious things and not the sort of subject that Morag thought should be discussed with a boy of Torquil's age. In any case, a witch in the family is a delicate matter and not the kind of thing that people care to talk about too much.

'Anyway,' said Torquil, 'the Trapper got no more than he deserved. He is a right bad one, that Alasdair.'

'So he is,' Morag agreed. 'But I will miss the kelpie, all the same.'

'Och, he'll come back again,' Torquil consoled her. 'He'll not be missing his blether with you over the head of Alasdair's foolishness.'

He went off to look after his animals, thinking of the story Morag had told him and how it showed the power that was in a little cross of rowan wood, and feeling more pleased than ever that he had one for himself. Morag, however, went about her work that day feeling very downcast at the thought that she would not see the kelpie again, and nobody was more pleased and surprised than herself when she went down to the pool that evening and saw the kelpie sitting there as usual.

It was soon clear, however, that he had not come in a friendly mood. As soon as Morag appeared he shouted at her,

'Why did you deceive me, old woman?'

'I did not deceive you!' she said, astonished.

'You never told me you were a witch,' the kelpie said angrily.

'You have no right to say that,' Morag said, feeling angry herself now. 'I am *not* a witch!'

'You used a witch's spell,' the kelpie retorted.

'Och, that!' she said. 'That was only an old rhyme I heard from my grandmother.'

'That is not true,' the kelpie shouted. 'It was a spell! Well you know it was a spell. And well you know the power of a rowan cross against people like us!'

'I am not a witch,' Morag insisted. 'And I'll thank you not to call me one. Anyway, there was no need to come here if you did not want to see me.'

'You wanted me to come, didn't you?' the kelpie demanded.

Morag nodded.

'Well then,' he said, 'I had to come. When a witch defeats one of us we have to come when she calls and do her bidding whether we like it or not. And I am here tonight because you wanted me to be here. That *proves* you are a witch.'

Morag shook her head sadly for she could see it was no use trying to convince the little man. 'Kelpie,' she said, 'it does not really matter whether or not you think I am a witch, but I've no wish to see someone who comes to speak to me only because he must and not because he wants to. Good night, kelpie, and good-bye.'

'Wait, wait!' the kelpie cried.

Morag looked down at him and saw that his small old face was all puckered up, whether it was with rage or something else she could not tell, and so she waited and the kelpie said,

'Tell me why you sent that man down to my pool.'

'He came of his own accord,' said Morag. 'I would never send anyone to torment you.' And she told him how it was that Alasdair had come to try and get the pearls from the pool.

The kelpie let go her bucket when she had finished.

'It seems you are not to blame after all,' he said. Then he gave Morag another of his odd, puckered-up looks. 'Like it or not,' he said, 'you have the power to call me to your side. But I would have come tonight in any case. You are not the only one on the hill-side that is lonely for times gone past.'

'Say no more,' said Morag gently. 'If you wish to think I am a witch, that is your affair. But I am glad you came, you are glad to be here, and that is all that matters.'

'Very well then,' the kelpie said. 'Let us talk of other matters.'

Morag smiled at him and laid her bucket down. 'Yes, let us talk of other things,' she agreed. She sat down on the bank and began to talk and so, in the end, the evening passed as pleasantly for the two of them as any other had done.

It was in this way that Morag and the kelpie mended their quarrel and he never said to her again that she was a witch (at least, not until a great deal later). Morag herself put the whole business out of her mind and it never occurred to her that Alasdair the Trapper had put the story of her spell on the kelpie round the whole of Abriachan.

The talk was of nothing else among the crofters on the next weekly bus to Inverness. The older folk re-called stories of Morag's grandmother. 'Blood will tell,' they said, shaking their heads. 'Fancy her being a witch and nobody ever suspected.' But the driver of the bus was a young man, and moreover, he was a modern man that did not believe in kelpies and he laughed to himself to hear them talking like this.

Now Inverness is a small town and you would not think that anything that was talked of there would be of interest anywhere else. But the truth of the matter is that thousands of people spend their holidays in the Highlands of Scotland every year and a great many of them come to Inverness. You can meet people from all parts of the world there any day in the summer time, and of course they all come there thinking the Highlands is a strange and wonderful place and naturally they are looking for the strange and wonderful things that are supposed to happen there.

So it was, as the weeks went by, that in the shops and hotels and in the office of the Tourist Board people from all over the world began to hear the story of Morag and Alasdair and the kelpie. Not that one of them believed it, mind you. They were all too clever and modern to believe such nonsense! But it stuck in their minds all the same, *It is only in the Highlands of Scotland you would hear such a thing,* they wrote proudly to their friends at home, and when all the other things happened later that the newspapers made such a fuss about, they all remembered the story and some of them claimed to have known from the beginning that Morag was a witch.

The one thing that nobody knew about, and that was because Alasdair never mentioned it, was the kelpie's pearls. When people asked him how he had come to be in the water in the first place he said he had tripped and fallen in, and like it or not they had to believe him for he would give them no further informaton. And so Alasdair kept the secret of the pearls, and many a time he thought about them and wondered how he could outwit the kelpie and get them for himself.

CHAPTER 4

The Monster

THE children had got their summer holidays from the school by this time and so, as Torquil was not going into town every day, he had no chance to hear all the gossip about Morag. He heard nothing of it from the people on the hill either, for all his time was taken up with the work the Woman gave him to do on her croft, with visits to Morag herself and with a new ploy that had begun with his study of a wild-cat's lair – the same one he had discovered the previous summer.

Most people would have called it a daft ploy because the wild-cat of the Scottish Highlands is one of the fiercest animals in the world and Torquil's idea was to try to tame one of the kittens of the litter that had just been born in the lair. Daft or not, however, he went about it in a sensible way.

First of all he went over the hill to the village of Kiltarlity where the man people called the Naturalist had his house. He was a famous man, the Naturalist. He wrote books about animals and made films of them and at first he was inclined to laugh at Torquil's plan, for even he had never succeeded in taming a wild-cat kitten. However, when he had had a taste of Torquil's skill in handling some of his own collection of animals he agreed to help him bag a kitten and pen it in one of the big wire cages at the back of his house.

Three weeks after its capture, Torquil was able to touch the kitten without the fierce little creature snarling and striking out at him and the Naturalist had to admit that he had a fair chance of success with his scheme.

'And if you *can* do it,' he said, 'there's nothing I wouldn't put past you where animals are concerned.'

He stroked his thick brown beard and looked down from his great height at Torquil crouching beside the wild-cat kitten. 'This collection of mine is getting a bit big for one man to handle,' he remarked. 'I've been thinking I'll need to be training up a lad to help me with it.'

'I'll help you,' Torquil said eagerly. 'I'll come every day after school.'

The Naturalist shook his head. 'I'm sorry, boy,' said he. 'I would need someone who would live here with me and take this sort of work up as a career. Now, if the Woman would let you do that . . . ?'

This time it was Torquil's turn to shake his head for he knew well that the Woman meant him to be a crofter like the rest of the people on the hill.

'Oh well, I'll maybe persuade her different,' the Naturalist said when Torquil told him this. 'It's a pity talent like yours should be wasted. We'll give it to the end of the holidays – then I'll have a word with her.'

Torquil ran back to the Woman's house with wings on his heels that day, thinking of what the Naturalist had said, but he was brought back to earth with a thud when he got there. The Woman had been away shopping in the town and there she had heard all the talk about Morag. She could talk of nothing else but what a terrible business it was and such a shame on the people of the hill to have such goings-on in their midst.

'And you that's always wandering the hill by yourself,' she finished, 'you be wise and do not go near the cailleach's house. She is a witch, mind, and dear knows the harm she could do you.'

'She is *not* a witch!' Torquil protested.

'Her grannie was one,' the Woman said. 'Everybody on the hill knows that.'

'I don't care what her grannie was!' Torquil shouted, quite forgetting his manners in his anger. 'Mistress Morag is a good woman!'

'Is that a way to talk to your elders?' the Woman snapped. 'And what do *you* know about it anyway, pray?'

Torquil's heart jumped into his mouth for he saw that by defending Morag he had nearly betrayed his own secret to the Woman.

'I am sorry,' he said meekly, and was greatly relieved when all she said was, 'Do not crow so loud then, my young cockerel, or I will clip your wings for you.'

Still, it grieved him that Morag should be talked of in this way and many times after that he was on the point of telling her about it and begging her to be careful not to give people like Alasdair any more chance to spread tales about her. Day after day he climbed up the hill meaning to speak words of warning to her, but every time he came in sight of the bright burn purling down the hill and smelt the piercing sweet scent of the white rose-bushes round her house he felt himself being drawn through the secret door of the dream-world at the top of the hill.

Everything changed places then. It was the dream-world that was real and the town below became like a dream – a dark dream that would cast a shadow over Morag's happiness if he let the chatter of evil words about her break through the secret door.

'What shall I do?' he asked the Naturalist one day. 'Should I tell her?'

'Ach, let the old woman be at peace,' said he. 'What good would it do to disturb her with something that will only be a nine-days wonder when all is said and done?'

And so Torquil said nothing, and all unaware that Alasdair had sown the seed of the trouble that was to grow so thick and fast about her, Morag was left in peace to enjoy her evenings with the kelpie beside the pool.

It happened to be a very fine summer that year, and with the long, light evenings you get up north in the summer-time they had plenty of time to sit and talk. The kelpie was very curious about Morag's witch-grandmother, and he being in quite a different case from Torquil in this respect, she was quite willing to tell him all she could remember about the old woman; how she used to tie red thread round the horns of her

45

cow and hang a branch of the rowan-tree over the byre door to protect it from the fairies, and how she used to light the great bonfires that were burned every year on the hill at Beltane in May and Hallowe'en in October, naming all the different kinds of wood that were used for the fire as she built it up.

'There were nine kinds of wood,' said Morag, 'willow, hazel, alder, birch, ash, yew, elm, holly and oak, and every wood had a secret meaning and purpose. But only my grandmother knew what they were. And four times a year she baked a cake that was called a quarter-cake for it was made each quarter-day at Candlemas, Beltane, Lammas and Hallowe'en. Then she would go out on to the hill-side and break the cake into pieces. She threw the pieces away as far as she could throw them, one by one, and as she threw them she cried,

'Here to thee, wolf, spare my sheep. Here to thee, fox, spare my lambs. Here to thee, eagle, spare my goats. Here to thee, harrier, spare my chickens.'

'And so she would keep all safe about her till the next quarter-day for there was a magic in that cake only herself knew the secret of making.'

'She sounds to me like a very wise woman,' said the kelpie.

'She was what they called a white witch,' Morag told him. 'She never used her power to harm anyone that I ever heard of.'

'Whatever she was,' said the kelpie, 'she had sense enough to see that there is more in the world around her than meets the eye, and that is more than you can say for most people.'

'True enough,' agreed Morag. 'There are not many people nowadays who can see further than the end of their nose. I doubt if there are many people who would even believe there is such a thing as a kelpie.'

'That is their loss!' the kelpie growled.

'Indeed and it is,' said Morag, taking her pail of water and getting ready to go back to the house.

She stood for a minute looking down at Loch Ness sparkling in the valley between the Abriachan hill-side and the Monadhliath Mountains. It is a big loch, Loch Ness, and deep – so deep that they say there are parts of it where no diver could touch the bottom. Morag stood thinking of this as she looked to right and left along the loch and suddenly she said,

'But you know, kelpie, some of these people that would not believe the evidence of their own eyes if they saw you, will swear that they have seen the monster that is supposed to live in the loch. Yet here am I who have lived for seventy-three years within sight of the loch and I have never once seen the monster. I think maybe it is their own imagination these people are seeing!'

'Then you are an old fool!' snapped the kelpie. 'The monster, as you call the creature, was living in the loch before my time and that is long enough as I have told you.'

Now when the kelpie talked like this Morag pretended to be offended, but she was secretly delighted, for this was what she had been leading up to the whole time. She had always been disappointed that she had never been able to get a sight of the monster that so many other people claimed to have seen, and so now she led the kelpie on by arguing that it was all a lot of nonsense.

'How can you *prove* it is there?' she asked.

'I'll show you!' the kelpie shouted, jumping up in a rage. 'You be there by the boat-pier at the loch-side tomorrow, and if you do not take back what you have just said you will be as stupid as Alasdair the Trapper.'

'I'll be there, kelpie,' Morag said meekly, but she had a job to keep her face straight after the way she had tricked him into saying just what she had wanted him to say. The little man was not so clever as he thought he was!

The next day was a Tuesday which was very convenient, as that was the day the weekly bus ran from Abriachan to Inverness, and it would not only take her to the loch-side, it would also save her legs the steep climb back up the hill. At four o'clock the next day, then, she got up to milk the cow and collect the eggs from the hens. She had her breakfast, tidied the house and dressed herself in her good black dress. Then she put some oatcakes, butter, cheese and milk into a basket, collected her knitting and set off to walk the half-mile across the heather to the road that ran down the hill.

There were two or three people waiting at the side of the road for the bus. They gave her a pleasant good morning and began to talk about the dry summer that was in it and how it was good for the hay and bad for the root-crops and such-like farming talk. Then one of them said,

'It is a strange thing to be seeing you go down to the big town, Mistress MacLeod. I cannot mind the last time you did that.'

'Och, it's so long ago, neither can I,' said Morag, 'but I am not going to Inverness at all this time. I am just going down to the loch to see the monster.'

Everybody smiled, thinking she was making a joke, and somebody said, 'It is a pity you cannot be sure of seeing it and you taking all the bother of going down to the loch.'

'Oh, I am sure to see it,' said Morag, who never saw any use in a lie where the truth would serve, 'for I spoke to a kelpie who promised me it would be there today.'

A strange look came over their faces when she said that and it was plain to see they thought she was out of her mind. When the bus came they went aboard whispering to one another, and as it went down the hill collecting more passengers at every stop, the whisper went round the newcomers as well.

'*Did you hear what the cailleach said? She's going down to the loch to see the monster. A kelpie told her it would be there, she said. Aye, poor soul, she's out of her wits.*'

So they all agreed among themselves, and when she got off the bus where it turned left into the main road to

Inverness they watched her curiously as she went down the grassy bank to the pier at the loch-side. Morag knew fine they were watching her and maybe talking about her too, but she was not in the least disturbed.

'What I do and how I do it is my own business,' she said.

And had no idea how wrong she would be proved before the day was out!

The bus went on to Inverness. It stopped at the bus station, the passengers scattered to the shops and the market, and soon the whisper was going round the town.

'*A cailleach that has lived on the hill-side all her life . . . says the monster will be seen today . . . a witch, they say . . . the old woman that set the horse on to Alasdair the Trapper . . . said it was a kelpie . . .*'

The whisper went round the shops and hotels and cafés. They heard it in the office of the Tourist Board and in the bus-station where holiday visitors to the town were waiting to buy tickets for bus tours. And soon the visitors began to ask questions, and more and more of them bought tickets for a circular tour of Loch Ness until the bus company had no more buses left to spare for the trip and had to refuse the bookings of those who came last.

The disappointed ones hired cars and bicycles and some even decided to go on foot in the hope of getting a lift, for there is not a single visitor to that part of the Highlands who does not hope to get a sight of the monster that is supposed to live in Loch Ness and those who were there that day were determined not to miss the chance.

Now it happened – as you might have seen in the newspapers at that time – that a great scientific expedition to find the monster had been got up that summer, and the whisper about Morag even reached the hotel room where all the scientists were working on their charts and instruments.

'Do you think, professor,' said one of them, 'that there is any truth in this rumour that is going round the town?'

The leader of the expedition was a very sensible modern man, and being a professor, of course, he had no time for such nonsense as kelpies.

'The Highlanders are a very superstitious people,' said he, 'always talking about ghosts and spirits and second-sight and suchlike nonsense. I think the old woman's monster-hunt will turn out to be a wild-goose chase!'

Everybody laughed at the professor's little joke and they all went back to their charts and instruments and thought no more about the whisper.

Morag, meanwhile, was enjoying herself by the edge of the loch. She had found a comfortable hummock to rest her back on and the sun was shining on her face like a blessing. 'I'm a lazy old woman,' she said to herself with a smile, and brought out her knitting. She had no need to look at the stocking she was making. Her hands flew along the needles with the skill of a lifetime and so she could watch the loch as she worked. When she got hungry she had some oatcakes and milk and then went back to her knitting.

A passenger steamer went up the loch, a canoe, and then a speedboat. Morag waved to the people on the steamer and they waved back to her. The boy in the canoe and the man in the speedboat never looked up, and Morag thought what a waste of a fine day it was to sail on deep blue water between high green mountains with never an eye for the glory around you.

She watched the gulls dipping and gliding into the eye of the sun so that they looked like silver arrows flashing across the sky, and felt very content with life and with herself. She was not in the least worried that the monster had not appeared as yet. The kelpie had promised her it would come and she was sure it would.

It was getting well along into the afternoon when she noticed that there seemed to be a great number of cars and buses and bicycles passing along the road, even for that time of the year, but she had no idea that the people in them were looking for her till she stood up to stretch her legs and saw people waving and shouting and pointing cameras at her.

'The very idea!' she said indignantly, sitting down again and wondering what they were all up to.

A young man in a bus-driver's uniform came down the bank from the road and said to her. 'Are you the lady that is waiting to see the monster?'

'That is what I am here for,' Morag said, very dignified. 'Why else should I spend a day idle at the loch-side when I have work to do on my croft?'

'Very true, mistress,' agreed the bus driver who was a Highlander himself and recognized the sense of her remark. 'I hope you'll not be minding all these people coming along to have a look at it too.'

'Not if they keep quiet and behave themselves like Christian people,' said Morag. 'You tell them that, young man, and I shall be obliged to you.'

The bus driver went away back up the bank and did as Morag had told him, and there was something so dignified about the old woman sitting there in her black dress and calmly getting on with her knitting that the visitors did just what she had told them to do.

Soon the loch-side was as peaceful as before with only the purr of the traffic on the road to disturb the silence and a steady murmuring sound like a hive of bees on a hot day, and that was the sound of all the people talking in whispers among themselves. And gradually, as the sun swung round to the west, the waters of the loch took on a darker blue and the setting sun laid a bright gold trail across it.

It was in this path of sunlight that the monster appeared. One moment there was nothing but the blank gold of the ripples dancing, and the next, there was a dark spot among them. The dark spot rose above the water; three more dark patches appeared in line with it among the ripples. From the crowd there came a long sighing sound and somewhere among them a child's voice shrieked, *The Monster!*

Morag sat watching it, entranced. It began to move

in an easterly direction raising a great flurry of water behind it, its head swaying and the humps behind it rising and falling the way a snake's body does. Then it turned inshore and began to swim in a diagonal line to where Morag was sitting. It came to within thirty yards of her. She could see it clearly – the long neck, the short blunt head, the wide mouth. The sun struck sparkles of light from the greyish humps of its back and she thought, 'It must be scales like a fish that's on it, surely, to make it sparkle so.'

Then the monster altered course till it was swimming west, parallel with the edge of the loch. Now it looked black against the sun. It dived. Morag scanned the blank surface of the loch. The crowd murmured with disappointment, then they roared as it surfaced again a hundred yards out. The head and one of the humps showed above the surface for a moment, then they disappeared and there was only the dark blue water with the sunlight trail fading from it and the gulls dipping and gliding above it.

'Well I'm blessed!' said Morag. 'Well I'm blessed! That kelpie is a remarkable creature, surely.'

She rose stiffly to her feet, collected her knitting and her basket and looked up to the road. There was a terrible confusion going on there, a great roar of talk and buses and cars revving up and all trying to pull out on to the road at once. A young man came leaping down to her. He had a camera on his back, a notebook in his hand, and his hair was standing on end.

'I'm from the *Inverness Journal*, Mistress McLeod,'

he said breathlessly. 'Will you give me a statement? How did you know the monster would be here?'

'Why, a kelpie told me, of course,' Morag said calmly. 'And now if you'll excuse me, young man, I must be getting away. I can see the Abriachan bus waiting at the corner and I've no notion to walk up the steep hill to my croft.'

And on she went as cool as could be, leaving the reporter looking quite bewildered. Nobody noticed her in all the confusion and excitement as she made her way through the crowd, but all the people on the Abriachan bus stopped their chattering as she climbed aboard and gave her the same strange looks they had given her in the morning. However, Highlanders are the most polite people on the face of the earth and they chatted pleasantly to her on the journey home. But nobody mentioned the monster.

Morag went down to the pool as usual that evening and found the kelpie waiting for her.

'Did you see the monster then?' he called as she came down the path.

'I did,' said Morag, 'and it was a remarkable sight, indeed it was.'

'Ha!' he boasted. 'There's a thing *you* couldn't do – bring the monster up like that just on the word of command!'

'Och, but I am just an ordinary old woman,' said she, laughing.

She settled down then to telling the kelpie everything that had taken place; the beautiful day that was in it and the peaceful quiet of the loch-side; how the monster had appeared, what it had looked like, and how the word had got around so that great crowds of people had come to see if it would appear.

The kelpie looked curiously at her while she was speaking. When she had finished he said,

'Mark my words, there's trouble ahead for you, mistress. You will not be "just an ordinary old woman" for much longer.'

He took good night of her and slipped back into the pool, leaving Morag wondering just what he had meant by this strange speech.

CHAPTER 5

The Book of
Elizabeth MacLeod

NOW the reporter who had spoken to Morag on the loch-side was a clever young man, and a well-educated one too, for he had been to the University of Edinburgh and had letters after his name. But of course, they don't teach you anything about kelpies at the University, and moreover the young man was a Lowlander and so his education had been quite neglected in this respect. He had no idea what Morag was talking about when she said to him that the kelpie had told her the monster would appear that day, and so on the bus back to Inverness he asked an old man sitting beside him what a kelpie was.

'Have you never heard of the kelpie?' asked the old fellow, quite amazed at his ignorance. 'The *Sasunnach*, the Lowlander, here, he's never heard of the kelpie!' he called to the rest of the folk on the bus – but of course he spoke in the Gaelic so as not to hurt the young man's feelings. Then, in English, he said to the young reporter, 'Well now, I'll tell you about the kelpie, and you be heeding my words if you are going to live in the Highlands! The kelpie is a water-spirit, and there is not a river or loch in the Highlands but has a kelpie living in it. But when the kelpie comes out of the water it takes the shape of a big black horse, and it is a very fierce creature indeed.'

The young man didn't believe such nonsense of course and he said, 'Have you ever seen a kelpie then?'

'Seen one!' cried the old fellow. 'I was as near as could be *drowned* by a kelpie once!'

Everybody on the bus was listening now, for Highlanders dearly love a story. The old man knew this very well and he settled himself down to the telling of it, quite pleased with all the attention he was getting.

'It happened by the River Garry,' said he, 'when I was only a wee boy. I was guddling a trout out from under a stone, and all at once I saw the kelpie's face in the water. My hair stood on end I can tell you, for it was a face as old as Time and wiser than all the books ever written. The next thing I knew, something grabbed one of my hands and tugged but I gave a great pull in the opposite direction and rolled back on the bank out of harm's way. Then what should rise out of the river but a great black horse, all gleaming-wet and eyes as red as coals. It climbed out on the bank and stood there dripping water and looking sideways at me out of those red eyes. I jumped to my feet meaning to run a mile from it, but it stood there quite quiet and peaceful beside me. Well, I was only a little lad then you understand, and this was a great fine horse and the notion came on me that it would be a grand thing to have a ride on its back. And mind you, I got the idea from the way the kelpie looked at me that it wanted me to do just that. "What's the harm!" said I, feeling what a bold lad I was, and I laid hold on its mane. I was just going to pull myself on to its back when I remembered what my mammy had said to me once. "Hamish," she said, "don't you ever ride the kelpie if you should meet with one, for it is a wicked creature that will carry you down to its home beneath the water and you'll never see your mammy again!" Well, when I remembered that, I let go the kelpie's mane and ran away as hard as I could. I only looked back once and that was enough. The kelpie was striking the ground with its hooves in such a rage that it put the fear of death in me and I ran all the way home shouting for my mammy.'

'And that,' said the old man, 'was how I was near drowned by the kelpie. And if you take my advice, young man, you'll do the same as I did if you should ever meet with one.'

The young man didn't know what to make of this at all and he thought maybe the old fellow was having a joke at him. However, he thought he might as well tell him what Morag had said about the kelpie.

'Morag MacLeod, did you say,' said the old man. 'Aye, she might well have had dealings with a kelpie. There's some say she is a witch and maybe she is at that. Why else would a kelpie be friendly with her? Depend upon it, they're two of a kind and likely up to no good.'

The reporter looked down his nose at the old man, thinking he was wandering in his wits. 'A witch!' said he. 'Now you *are* talking nonsense!'

'Maybe aye, maybe no,' said the old man. 'But her

grannie was a witch, that's for certain sure. She cured my knee of warts with a powerful charm when I was a wee boy.'

'She charmed the milk back into one of my grandad's cows that had gone dry,' said a young woman in the next seat.

'And found a silver crown-piece that my grannie had lost when no one else could find it,' said another passenger.

And so they went on talking all round the young man about Morag and her grannie and the kelpie, and him sitting there thinking what a curious business it all was and making up in his head the piece he was going to write about Morag in the newspapers.

When he got back to his office he sat down and wrote it all out and sent it off with a photograph he had taken of Morag and another of the monster to a big Edinburgh newspaper. And there it appeared the next day, and a very strange tale it made too – all about Morag being a witch with a familiar spirit that prophesied things to her, and how she and the kelpie had made a spell to bring the monster up out of the loch for everyone to see.

This roused a great deal of curiosity naturally, and people began coming up the hill to have a look at the cause of it all. They came in ones and twos first, then in dozens and finally in hundreds, for the first ones who came saw more than they had bargained for and they spread the tale of that too.

What they had seen was Morag with Torquil's animals. She was sitting out in the sunshine in her little garden peeling vegetables for a pot of broth, and because it was such a fine morning she had taken the animals out of their cages to give them an airing and to keep her company. Dondo the blackbird was on his favourite perch on her head and one of the little hamsters was sitting on her lap washing his face with his paws the careful way hamsters do; the other animals were scattered about the grass enjoying the fresh green shoots and Polar was curled at her feet with his fierce ferret-eyes closed against the bright sunshine.

It was the kind of thing that Torquil and Morag herself took as a matter of course, but to the townspeople who came to see her it was a thing of wonder and even of fear. Even those who were country-bred looked on in awe to see a fierce creature like a polecat ferret lying peacefully beside creatures that were its natural prey. One and all they jumped to the conclusion that here was proof before their eyes of Morag's strange powers, and so the story grew even further.

In no time at all the editors of other papers were asking what strange business this was going on up in the Highlands and sending reporters to find out. They came up the hill road to Abriachan in their cars and then came stumbling across the heather in their city shoes to Morag's door and asked her questions till her head rang. Then they went back to Inverness and asked the professor who was the leader of the scientific expedition to find the monster what he thought of it all.

Well naturally, the professor being a scientific man

didn't believe a word of anything that had happened, and when the reporters asked him, 'Do you think Mistress MacLeod is a witch?' he said, 'I think she is a humbug!'

Now this was not a very nice thing to say, but then maybe he was a bit annoyed about an ordinary old

woman like Morag getting all the attention instead of having his scientific expedition written about in the newspapers.

It made no difference to the reporters anyway. They still wrote stories about Morag in their newspapers, and when she got tired of answering their questions they spoke to other people at Abriachan and collected tales of Morag's witch-grandmother. In fact, the only thing they didn't manage to find out about was the pearls in the Kelpie's pool, for Morag was too afraid of having the pool disturbed again to risk mentioning them and Alasdair, of course, had his own reasons for keeping quiet about the pearls.

The Witch of Abriachan they called Morag in their newspapers, and soon everybody was talking about her and wondering was she or wasn't she a witch. 'How else would she know the monster would appear that day?' asked those who thought she was, and so the argument went on. No one outside of the Highlands believed her story about the kelpie, of course, but those who did believe it were all the more certain that she must be a witch, especially those who had seen her with Torquil's animals.

Torquil, of course, blamed himself for all this. 'If only I'd warned her in the beginning,' he thought, 'she would not have risked talking about the kelpie to anyone!'

When he realized how his animals had added to the stories about Morag he was even more sorely vexed and would have shouted it aloud to everyone that they belonged to him, but Morag would not allow him to say a word.

'Do you want to put a death sentence on the innocent creatures?' she asked sternly. 'Because that is just what you will do if the Woman ever learns the truth.'

There was no doubt that this would be the case if the Woman ever learnt the animals had been the cause of his disobeying her order not to go near Morag. Once

Torquil had admitted this to himself he went in fear that she would find out about them, and so for both of them things went from bad to worse as the days went by.

The people who came to look at Morag and the kelpie's pool camped all over the hill-side. They stared at her whenever she went out, frightened her hens and scattered her sheep and altogether quite destroyed her peace. She took to going down to the pool after dark to draw water, and through the day Torquil tried to save her from the worst of the curiosity by doing all the outside work of the croft. But still, it was a terrible time for Morag and a lonely time too, for of course the kelpie never showed his face while all this was going on.

The fine weather held all this time and each morning Morag would stand in her doorway looking down at the sparkling water of the loch and wishing that the weather would break. 'A storm would drive them all off the hill-side,' she would sigh, searching the sky for signs of bad weather. But the sky stayed blue and the sun shone as brightly each day as on the day before.

'I wish I could *make* a storm!' said Morag, exasperated, one morning as she looked out on another cloudless day. The words were hardly out of her mouth before the thought came to her that she knew where to get the answer to her wish.

There was a little old black cupboard built into the wall of her kitchen, and that cupboard had belonged to her grandmother. Inside it were things that only her grandmother knew about and no one else had ever dared to look at or to touch. The answer to her wish was inside that cupboard!

Morag turned from the door and went into the kitchen. She took a key off its hook on the wall and stood looking down at the little old black cupboard. It had never been opened since her grandmother died and her heart beat loudly when she thought of what she would find inside it. Then she thought of all the noise and fuss that would soon be stirring on the hill-side and with trembling fingers she put the key in the lock and turned it.

The door of the cupboard swung open and a smell came from inside it, a smell that Morag could not place. Her knees began to shake again but she bent down to the cupboard and lifted out a big book that took up nearly the whole of one shelf. It was bound in black leather and as she lifted it out she realized that it was the mustiness of this leather binding she had smelt when the door of the cupboard swung open. For all that, though, the book was in truly amazing condition for its great age.

Morag had never seen this book before, though she had heard plenty about it, and it was with a feeling of great awe that she turned over the thick yellow pages written all over in her grandmother's hand. It was all in the Gaelic, of course, but Morag could read and write that language as well as speak it and once she had got used to the cramped style of the writing in the book she managed very well.

There was nothing on the first page except

Elizabeth MacLeod
Her Book of Magic

but every page after that was closely written on. Morag's eye skimmed over the heading of each page.

A spell for the Raising of a Fair Crop. For the Finding of Things that be Lost, Ane Powerful Spell. Ane Charm for the Taking-away of Enchantment over Cattle-beasts

she read – and so on. There seemed to be a spell for everything except the raising of a storm, but at last she found it and settled down to read it carefully.

For the Raising of a Storm take first a piece of linen cloth that has been neither washed nor worn but is fair and clean, and of colour, white. Take also four pieces of green wool of equal length. A Powder of Spiders' Blood. Four each of the Jewel in the Forehead of a Toad. Four feathers from the breast of a white cock. And a Pitcher of Water from a kelpie's pool. Lay these things before you and do thus with them.

So her grandmother had written.

Morag stopped reading in dismay at this point. She could supply the cloth, the wool, the feathers and the water from the kelpie's pool, but where would she find a powder of spiders' blood and the forehead jewels of four toads?

She rose from the table where she was sitting with the book of magic in front of her and went over to her grandmother's cupboard. Except for the space where the book had been, the three shelves of it were full of little brown stone jars and wooden boxes, each with a label on it. There was nothing for it but to look and see if one or more of these held what she needed, and she began to take them out carefully one by one.

Some of the labels were hard to read, some she could not read at all and she was almost in despair when, right at the back of the shelf, she found a tiny jar labelled Ane Powder of the Blood of Spiders. A few minutes after this she picked up a small box that rattled and on the label of it she read The Forehead Jewels of Certain Toads.

She opened both cautiously. The spiders' blood was a dark brown powder, and the jewels looked to her like tiny, yellowish-brown stones. Greatly relieved that she could go on with the spell now that she had all the things she needed, she went back to the book.

Grind small the jewels into the spiders' blood, and make with this a paste, using the water from the kelpie's pool. Take then the four white feathers and cover them with this paste, and wrap each feather into a corner of the white cloth, tying each tightly in its place with a piece of the green wool. Take then this cloth between midnight and dawn of the day the storm is desired to begin to a boundary stone where the land of three lairds meet, and lay it on the boundary stone. And with a branch of rowan tree beat the cloth as it lies on the boundary stone, all the time saying,

> I beat this charm upon this stane,
> To raise the wind, to bring the rain,
> They shall not lie till I please again.

Morag raised her head and whispered the words of the rhyme to herself and she shivered, but it was excitement that shook her now instead of the fear that had gripped her before. Her fingers tingled where they touched the book of magic, and it seemed to her that the words on its yellow pages had begun to glow as if they had been traced there by a fiery pen that had left them still smouldering through all the years they had lain in the little old black cupboard.

She looked down at the writing below the rhyme.

When cloth has been beaten and the spell cast, bury the cloth on the west side of the boundary stone and cast the rowan branch into running water, saying,

> Rowan-tree, harm not me,
> On my foes this storm shall be.

Within one hour from sunrise after this the storm shall break and shall continue for three days thereafter, and shall cease at dawn on the fourth day.

And I, Elizabeth MacLeod, being a white witch who has harmed no one with her power, do conjure any who read this book not to cast this spell for destruction and malice, but only for the protection of the weak. And if they do as I command, the storm will pass over and above them and they will receive no harm from it. But whoso casts this spell in malice, my curse shall fall on them and they will be destroyed in the storm that will arise from the spell.

'Well, that's plain enough,' said Morag as she read this warning. 'It's lucky for me my conscience is clear!'

Just then she heard Torquil's footsteps outside at the back of the house as he arrived to go about his work. Quietly she closed the book, put it back on the shelf with the little jar and the box and locked the cupboard again. Then she filled the kettle and put it on the fire and when Torquil came in she was sitting waiting for him with the tea-pot ready at her elbow.

First of all she gave him a chance to drink his tea. Then, 'Torquil,' she said, 'I have found a way to get rid of all those people that are destroying the peace of the hill-side.'

Torquil gave her a serious look and asked, 'And how can you do that, Mistress Morag?'

Now Morag had already made up her mind not to tell him this because she was not sure yet that she could make the spell exactly as it said in her grandmother's book and she knew that the smallest thing wrong with a spell means it will not work.

'Time enough to say when it is done,' she told him, 'but if my plan works it means you will not be able to come up here for the next three days.'

'Yes I can, I'm still on my school holidays,' said Torquil.

'You will not be able to come because of what I am going to do,' Morag explained.

'But my animals,' he protested. 'Who will feed them?'

'I will,' Morag said. 'No harm will come to them, Torquil. No harm will come to anyone, I promise you.'

Torquil looked away from her, not saying a word. He had grown up a great deal in the past few weeks the way boys do all of a sudden when they are twelve or so, and he was beginning to understand that he was the only one who could see the two sides of the argument about Morag.

He knew very well that there really was a kelpie in the pool because he had seen it for himself. He knew very well also that strange beings such as the kelpie have strange powers and so he saw no reason to doubt Morag's story that he had brought the monster up for her to see. And he knew best of all that there was no witchcraft about the gift of King Solomon's Ring that he shared with her. Still, he understood how strange the whole business must appear to those who did not know her as he did. He began to try to explain this to Morag but she held up her hand to silence him.

'Look at me, Torquil,' she commanded.

Torquil looked up and met her eyes. They were old eyes with many lines and wrinkles round them, but old and tired as they were there was a light in them that could not be mistaken for anything else but the light of truth.

'I am not a witch whatever they say,' Morag said quietly. 'Do you believe me, Torquil?'

'Of course I believe you,' said he, looking at that steadfast light. But to himself he could not help adding with a sigh, 'But I am the only one that does.'

He went away soon afterwards and thinking of his sad and troubled face Morag sighed too as she collected the dishes and washed them. When everything was neatly back in its place she went to the little black cupboard again. She unlocked the door, took her grandmother's book from the shelf and put it on the kitchen table. Then she opened it at the proper place and was about to sit down to read the words of the spell again when there came a knocking at her front door, a knocking that grew louder and louder till it shook the house and nearly made her die of fright.

CHAPTER 6

The Dam and the Spell

IT was Alasdair the trapper who was doing all the knock-knock-knocking on Morag's front door and it was good fortune for Morag that she got her wits back in time to open it to him before it was broken in with the weight of his fists on it.

'Go away, Alasdair,' she said as soon as she saw who it was. 'I'm busy. I'm very busy.'

She started to close the door but Alasdair said, 'I must talk to you, mistress. Let me come in.'

This put Morag in a worse state of nerves than ever. 'You can't come in – no one can come in!' she cried.

'That's where you are wrong,' snarled the Trapper and stuck his foot in the door. Morag cried out in alarm at this and shut the door hard on his foot. The Trapper drew it back from the door with a howl of pain and Morag seized her chance to bang the door properly shut. She locked the door and bolted it, and still shaking with the fright he had given her, she went to the window and watched the Trapper limping away from the house.

At the burn he stopped for a minute and stared at the kelpie's pool. Then he turned and shook an angry fist at her before he went on across the burn and down the hill. Morag shrank back from the window when he shook his fist but she was not too frightened to notice that Alasdair had none of his trapping gear with him, and if he was not out on his trapping rounds why had he come to her house?

Well, wondering only makes your head big, as they say, and Morag was too sensible to waste time puzzling over questions that had no answer and so without any more loss of time she turned from the window and went back to her grandmother's book of magic.

First of all she had to collect all the things she needed to make the spell. She went to her linen-chest and took from it a clean white linen napkin that had never been washed or used since the day it was made. She found green wool in her work-basket and then collected the toad-jewels and the spiders' blood from her grandmother's cupboard. Then she stepped cautiously outside the back door and picked up the white cock so quickly that he had hardly time to realize he had left the ground before she had plucked four white feathers from his breast. Last of all she fetched a pitcher of water from the pailful she had drawn the night before from the kelpie's pool, and the stone bowl called a 'knocking-stone' that she used for grinding the meal for her porridge.

Then, just as if she was going to do a baking, she laid all these things handy at one end of the kitchen table, put the book at the other end and the knocking-stone in the middle and began to make the spell.

It is important for everything about a spell to be performed in its proper order and so she was very careful to follow exactly the instructions in the book of magic. She sprinkled the powder of spiders' blood into the knocking-stone, dropped in four of the toad-jewels and ground them till they were all mixed together in a fine powder. On to this she measured water from the pitcher till she had enough in the knocking-stone to mix the powder to a paste.

When this was done she cut the green wool into four equal lengths and spread out the white cloth. Then she dipped the four white feathers into the knocking-stone. When they were coated evenly with the paste she laid them on the corners of the cloth, wrapped the corners round them and tied each one tightly into place with a piece of green wool, and the charm was made.

Morag worked slowly, but even so it was still early in the day when she finished. However, with all the excitement of it she was tired as if she had done a hard day's work and so she sat down to rest in her rocking-chair in front of the fire. She would need all her strength later, she knew, for the boundary stone where the land of three lairds met was four miles away and that is a long walk for an old woman at night and over rough hill ground.

For the rest of the day, then, Morag rocked and knitted and sometimes slept a little as old people do. People came to the door several times and knocked and called but she gave them no answer. None of the knocking was Alasdair's heavy thundering on her door and as the day wore on she decided she must have seen the last of him and his wild schemes for getting the kelpie's pearls. But in this, as she had been in wearing the pearls and in mentioning the monster, Morag was mistaken.

All this time, you see, that she had been 'in the head-lines' as the newspaper-men call it, Alasdair had never stopped thinking about the pearls and wondering how to get hold of them. It was a problem all right! No man in his senses would go into that pool again, and even if two or three men could work something out between them, sharing the risk meant sharing the profit. And anyway, who would take the first plunge?

'Not me!' thought Alasdair, shivering at the memory of the kelpie's great hooves plunging down to his head.

Of course, he could take a gun with him but even as he thought this Alasdair knew it was just as daft to think a bullet could kill the kelpie. A silver bullet? Well, they said you couldn't kill a witch except with a silver bullet, but a witch was still flesh and blood whereas a kelpie –

'Ach, there's no such thing as a kelpie!' Alasdair roared when he came to this point in his thinking.

And yet he was afraid to try for the pearls again *because* of the kelpie! It just didn't make sense.

The whole thing was driving him mad and that was why, on the same day that Morag decided to unlock her grandmother's cupboard (though he wasn't to know that, of course), he made up his mind to go and see her again and see if he couldn't tempt her to get the pearls for him.

'I'd share them with her,' he said, but this was a lie.

The Trapper was a bad-hearted man and he had no intention of sharing the pearls with anyone.

However, the scheme was all ready on the tip of his tongue to tell to Morag when she shut the door on his foot and left him outside the house howling with pain. If looks could have killed, then Morag would surely have dropped stone dead at the expression on Alasdair's face. But Morag was safe inside her house and there was nothing left for Alasdair to do but to limp away down the hill muttering angrily to himself, and that was what he did.

It was when he paused at the burn to glare at the kelpie's pool that the idea came to him that made him turn and shake his fist at Morag watching him from her window. Bad man or no, he was still a good trapper with his eyes open to all the signs of the weather and he noticed then that the water in the burn was very low with the lack of rain on the hill that summer. It struck him suddenly that if he could dam the burn at a point further up than the kelpie's pool, the water in it would drain off and leave it dry for him to collect the pearls!

'And the kelpie wouldn't be there!' he cried. 'It can only live in water!'

It was the answer to his problem and he ran all the rest of the way to the bothy where he kept his tools and collected a spade for digging, and some food. Back he went to the burn again full of his plans and eager to start work, and was greatly put out to find a tent with four men beside it by the very part of the burn he meant to dam. Two of the men were preparing a meal and another one was watching the loch through a pair of binoculars. The fourth one had a mirror in his hand and he was moving it up and down in the sun's rays so that it sent flashes back and forward.

The flashing mirror puzzled Alasdair. He looked round to see the reason for it and further along the hillside he saw the white dot of another tent. There were flashes coming from this one too, and presently he realized that the man with the mirror was signalling to someone at the other tent and getting a message back in the same way. Then the man with the binoculars turned to him and he recognized the professor who was leading the scientific party to find the monster, and it came to him that the tents were their observation posts for watching the loch.

This was a great blow. If he started damming the burn now all sorts of awkward questions would be asked. Scowling, he sat down behind a big rock to think of what he could do next.

From all he had heard, the professor's party meant to spend the whole summer on their investigations, and if he waited till they were gone for good someone might get the pearls before him, for with all the fuss about Morag and the kelpie someone would be sure to suggest the idea of draining the pool eventually.

No, decided Alasdair, the thing would have to be done now while only Morag and he knew about the pearls. But it would have to be done after nightfall when the professor and his men were asleep.

He settled himself down to watch and wait. From time to time he glanced towards Morag's cottage further down the burn but there was no sign of life from it. There was very little stir in the camp either. The men took turns at signalling and scanning the loch with binoculars but he soon got tired of watching this. The hot sun on the back of his neck and the murmuring of bees among the small moorland flowers made him feel drowsy. He yawned and thought to himself that there was nothing to be gained by staying awake. He lay back on the warm grass, his eyelids drooped, and he was asleep.

All over the hill-side the summer sun held everything in its sleepy haze. Even the chattering noise of the sightseers round Morag's house was hushed, and in the house itself Morag slept the light sleep of old people. And so the day crept on towards the testing time of night when Alasdair would begin to build his dam and Morag would set out to cast her spell, each of them thinking that what they had to do would be a race against time and neither of them knowing it would be a race against one another.

It was as dark as it was likely to be that night when Morag and Alasdair awoke, for it is never really true dark so far north in the summer. However late it is there is always a faint greenish glow on the horizon – a sort of false dawn that lasts the whole night through. The dawn, however, is about four o'clock at that time of the year, and when Morag looked at her grandfather clock and Alasdair at the watch in his waistcoat pocket, each of them reckoned that they had time to do what they had to do before sunrise.

Alasdair stood up behind his rock and Morag went to the door of her cottage. There were no lights in the campers' tents, no sign of life anywhere.

'I am the only person awake on the hill-side,' thought Morag.

'I am the only person awake on the hill-side,' thought Alasdair, and he rolled up his sleeves to start the job of building the dam.

Morag went back into her house. She poured herself a cup of soup from the pot simmering gently on the hob and quickly drank it down. Then she took the charm from the table where it had lain all day, put her shawl over her head and went out. The boundary stone lay on the same side of the burn as her house but first she had to go down to the burn to get a switch off the rowan-tree with which to beat the charm. She broke a thin light branch from the tree beside the kelpie's pool then turned and set off on her long walk to the boundary stone.

There was no path to the stone and it was rough going over the springy stems of the heather and through waist-high bracken. Morag had expected this, of course. She had allowed herself enough time to take things slowly and the excitement of the business in hand held her spirits up as she tramped along, but for all that she was soon foot-sore and weary. However, she reached the boundary stone at last, took the charm from her pocket, laid it on the stone and raised the rowan stick.

She was a queer figure standing there all alone on the dark slope of the hill-side – a small bent old woman with wisps of white hair sticking out from the black shawl round her head, the stick raised high and the charm glimmering white on the stone in front of her.

But Morag was not thinking of the way she looked. She was thinking of the thing she had to do, and now there was a fear on her that she could not name and she felt very lonely and very old. But there could be no turning back now. To leave a spell half-finished is a dangerous thing, as she knew. She clenched her fist on the stick, brought it down with a sharp smack on the cloth and cried,

> 'I beat this charm upon this stane,
> To raise the wind and bring the rain,
> They shall not lie till I please again.'

Whack! Whack! went the stick on the cloth as she spoke, and in the quietness of the night the blows sounded loud and clear.

Morag stopped, panting with the effort, and lifted the cloth off the stone. With the heel of her shoe and the point of the rowan stick she scraped a hole in the ground on the west side of the boundary stone, dropped the charm in and covered it up. Now there was only the stick to be cast away into running water and the spell would be finished.

'I'll throw it in the burn beside the house,' Morag decided.

She started off back the way she had come, and though it was light enough now to see her way, she was so tired that she stumbled as she went. She was so tired, in fact, that she went a bit wrong in her direction and it was not till she had been walking for a while that she realized she would come in sight of her house further up the burn than she had intended. However, she was too relieved at getting over the part of the spell she had done and too concerned with the business of throwing away the stick to let the mistake in direction worry her.

Meanwhile, things had not gone quite so well with Alasdair the Trapper as they had with her, although it had seemed at first that they would. There were any number of big boulders in and around the burn, and being a strong man he had soon gathered plenty to build a high enough wall for his dam. It was when he waded into the water to put them in position that the trouble started.

He needed both hands to hold the big boulders and so he had no way of steadying himself on the bed of pebbles worn smooth and slippery with the swift flow of the water. With the first of the big stones in his hands he slipped and fell full-length in the water, cracking his knee hard against a jutting rock as he fell.

He got to his feet, spluttering and shaking the water out of his hair and groaning at the jar of pain that shot down his leg. The boulder had rolled downstream but he set his teeth against the pain, limped down and got it and put it in position. Then out on to the bank for the next one he went, his ears straining for sounds from the tent in case all the splashing had wakened the professor and his men.

Nobody stirred there and Alasdair heaved the next stone into position, crawling into the water with it so that he wouldn't lose his footing again. Half-a-dozen more of the big boulders and the groundwork of the dam was in position, but by the time this was done he was shivering in his soaked clothes and his fingers were numb with cold. He could hardly feel the smaller stones

he fitted on top of the big ones, and when it came to
plugging the cracks that were left, the pebbles slipped
from his frozen fingers and kept falling back into the
bed of the burn.

But the Trapper was a stubborn man and a greedy
one, forbye. He meant to get the pearls whatever the
cost and so he laboured on at chinking the dam. The

sky began to lighten in the east and the water-level behind the dam was rising. All it needed now was packing with divots of grass from the bank.

Alasdair scrambled up the bank for his spade, never noticing in his haste the big trail of bramble in his way. His foot caught in it and he crashed to the ground with the hand that was grasping the side of the bank doubled under him. Pain pierced his forearm and he rolled over with a gasp. The sharp skinning-knife that he carried always at his belt had been jerked half out of its sheath as he fell and the blade had gone deep into his forearm.

Now, you could accuse the Trapper of a lot of bad things and be right in what you said, but being a coward wasn't one of them. He looked at the blood welling from the deep gash in his arm and he looked at the lightening sky and he made his choice.

If he stopped to bandage his arm now he would not be able to finish the dam before daybreak. There was still enough water seeping through to keep the kelpie's pool half-full and that meant he would have to wait another twenty-four hours to get the pearls, for the professor would use every minute of daylight there was for his spying on the loch.

He jumped to his feet, seized his spade and hacked away at the bank. The blood from his arm ran down the spade and dripped on to the grass but he cut and hacked away like a madman and paid no heed to it. The pile of divots grew till there was enough for his purpose. He gathered them in his arms, jumped down into the bed of the burn, packed them tight against the trickles of water – and the dam was finished!

Alasdair climbed wearily out on to the bank then, and the thought in his mind was that if any man had earned the pearls it was himself. He picked up his spade and stumbled over to the rock where he had slept the day before, and there he sat down and groped for his handkerchief to tie up his arm. The rim of the sun came over the horizon just as he was pulling the knot of the bandage tight with his teeth and his good hand and a few minutes later the flap of the tent was drawn aside and the professor stepped out.

He stood looking down to the loch for a minute and then he walked over to the burn. He saw the dam, stared at it in a puzzled way, and looked all around as if he was looking for a sign of who had built it. Alasdair was keeping well down behind his rock, of course, and the professor caught never a glimpse of him, but suddenly he started and bent down for a close look at the dam. He had seen the blood-stains on the divots of grass.

Alasdair watched him, grinning in spite of the pain in his arm at the puzzled expression on the professor's face, but the grin faded from his face as he saw someone coming across the hill a little way up the burn from him. It was a woman – an old woman, thought Alasdair, seeing the shawl round her head and the slow, stooping walk. The old woman came nearer and he saw that it was Morag.

A dozen thoughts flashed through his mind and the

foremost of them was *Where has she been? What has she been doing?* But before he could make up his mind what to do the professor had seen Morag too and was hurrying up the hill, waving and shouting to attract her attention.

CHAPTER 7

The Storm

IT was lucky for Morag after all that she had come out further up the burn than she had intended for of course the water had stopped flowing now below the point where the Trapper had dammed it. She saw the professor and heard him shouting to her just as she was about to cast the rowan stick into the burn. Quickly she tossed it in and said softly,

> 'Rowan tree, harm not me.
> On my foes this storm shall be.'

The stick floated off as she spoke and with a great sigh of relief that it was all over, Morag turned and waited for the professor to come up to her.

Now the professor had been doing a bit of thinking up there in his tent and it seemed to him that he might have been a bit hasty in calling Morag a humbug because, after all, she *had* seen the monster, and so, seeing that it was part of his job with the expedition to collect as many first-hand accounts of the creature as he could, he had decided it would do no harm to have a talk with her and listen to what she had to say.

'Providing,' he said to himself, 'that she doesn't start any of this nonsense about kelpies. I've no time to be bothered with fairy-tales!'

Well, he said all this as politely as he could when he got near enough to Morag to talk to her. She listened to him and said never a word till he was finished. Then, instead of talking about the monster, she said,

'Professor, there is going to be a storm. I think you would be better away from this hill.'

'A storm!' said he, looking round at the blue sky and the sun shining on the hill. 'My good woman, there's no sign of a storm!'

'There will be a storm within the hour,' said Morag flatly.

The professor looked at her as if he thought she was mad – which indeed he might be excused for thinking – but as he stood there staring, a black cloud came over the sun and a cold wind blew suddenly out of the east.

'The storm is coming,' Morag warned him again.

'But how did *you* know?' demanded the professor, for there was no denying now that the sky was taking on all the signs of a storm.

'I know because it was me that raised it,' said Morag.

'What!' shouted the professor, not believing the evidence of his own ears. 'You what?' he shouted again, turning his jacket-collar up as the wind brought rain whistling round his neck.

'I raised it,' repeated Morag calmly.

The whole sky had darkened now and the rain was beginning to pelt down.

'I raised it with a spell to drive all those strangers off the hillside and get peace for myself again.'

'You're crazy!' the professor screamed above the howling of the wind.

'I am not,' said Morag, and the professor noticed that he could hear her clearly though she spoke as quietly and calmly as before. And another curious thing he noticed. His own jacket was rapidly becoming soaked by the rain but Morag's dress and shawl were completely dry. The wisps of hair sticking out from her shawl were not even lifted by the wind that roared past his ears. He started to say something, changed his mind, and without another word started back down the hill to his tent as fast as he could go, with a look very like fear on his face.

A great gust of wind nearly carried him off his feet when he was half-way there, and as he stumbled about trying to get his balance again he saw his tent flap loose and break away from its ropes and the men who had been sleeping in it scrambling about in a great deal of confusion and alarm as the storm struck them.

All over the hill-side, drenched and scurrying figures were slackening tent-ropes and rescuing things that had been left to lie outside in the days of fine weather, and all the time the rain got heavier, the wind blew stronger, and the thunder began to crack and roll as if the sky was splitting. And Morag walked quietly homewards through all the confusion and calmly got on with the business of making the tea and boiling an egg for her breakfast.

From behind his rock where he lay clutching his wounded arm, the Trapper watched her go and cursed

his luck as he saw the level of the water in the burn rising. An hour of this rain, he reckoned, and the dam he had spent the whole night building would be swept away!

The hour came and went, and still the rain poured down. The divots tamped between the stones were washed away. The stones began to rock before the rushing force of the water. One toppled and broke free. A gush of water flowed through the gap it made, and as Alasdair stood there soaked to the skin and watching his dam crumble and topple altogether, the level of water in the kelpie's pool rose till the pearls were hidden again as deep as they had ever been.

When the Trapper saw this such a passion of rage gripped him that he started hurling big stones into the pool, quite forgetting in his temper about his wounded arm. Well, of course, this made it start bleeding all over again, and when Alasdair came to his senses and saw how the blood was pouring out of his arm he was fright-

ened out of his wits in case he would bleed to death.

He took to his heels and ran for dear life to Morag's house.

'Let me in, Mistress MacLeod!' he roared, hammering on the door with his good hand. 'Let me in before I bleed to death on your doorstep!'

The roaring and hammering brought Morag to her window with a frightened expression on her face, but as soon as she realized that Alasdair was hurt she opened the door to him and very quickly had his arm bandaged up as neatly as he could have had it done in a hospital. She had no sympathy for him, though, after the way he had behaved.

'I'll be bound this is all your own fault, Alasdair,' she said as she poured him a cup of tea.

'It was an accident,' Alasdair said sullenly. 'I slipped and fell on my skinning-knife when I was building a dam to drain the kelpie's pool.'

'So *that's* what you've been up to!' said Morag. 'Well, you can rest assured you've had all your trouble for nothing, my fine fellow, for there's no dam will stand up to the weight of water that's coming down the burn now!'

'I know that better than you,' Alasdair snarled. 'Haven't I just seen my dam crumble before my eyes?' He drank his tea and said, 'Just you wait though, mistress. I'll build another dam, and this time I won't have the bad luck to have it swept away by a storm.'

'It's not you will decide that,' Morag told him, but he was not listening to her.

'I'd best stay here till the storm's over,' he decided, watching the rain stream down the window.

'You will not!' said Morag sharply. 'The storm will last for three days and you're not staying in *my* house for three hours, never mind three days!'

Alasdair jumped to his feet and stood towering over her. 'How do *you* know the storm will last three days?' he demanded. 'How can *you* tell?'

Morag jumped to her feet too and faced up to him. 'Don't you try to bully me, Trapper,' she cried, 'and me after tying your arm up as good as a nurse in the hospital! Mind your own business!'

'This storm's come between me and my pearls!' shouted Alasdair. 'That makes it my business, and either you're guessing it will last three days or you're telling lies!'

'I don't need to guess and I never told a lie in my life,' Morag said scornfully. 'I know the storm will last for three days because I raised it with a spell that lasts for three days. Now be off with you!'

'*You* raised the storm?' Alasdair said stupidly. Fear flashed up in his eyes and he backed away from her with a face gone as grey as ashes. 'You're a witch!' he whispered, stepping back as if the floor had turned to tar and was sticking to the sole of his boots.

Morag looked at him steadily. 'I'm an old woman that's tired of greedy folk like yourself and curious folk like those that have been pestering me,' she said. 'Call me what you like so long as you leave me alone.'

Still Alasdair backed away till he was near enough

the door to make a grab for the latch. 'You *are* a witch!' he shouted as he jerked it open.

'Don't come back then!' Morag shouted after him.

As her voice came echoing to him through the wind and the rain Alasdair 'made horns' – as the country people call the sign that wards off the evil eye; that is, he clenched his right fist with the first and fourth fingers sticking out and pointing in Morag's direction. Then he stumbled away across the soaking grass and heather and on to the road, fear driving him all the time like a whip on his back. What with the wind lashing at him, however, and the rain beating cold on his head, his fear of Morag soon turned to black, bitter anger against her and schemes of revenge began to go through his head.

At the foot of the hill he saw a Land Rover and a trailer standing outside the house where Torquil and the Woman lived, and the two of them busy helping the driver of it to load the trailer with turnips. The man would likely be taking them into the town to sell, thought Alasdair, and he decided to seize the chance of a lift so that he could go to see a doctor about his arm. Thinking the way he did about Morag he was half-afraid by this time that she might have poisoned it with the dressing she had put on the wound!'

'Well, Alasdair,' the Woman greeted him when he stopped at the gate, 'it's terrible weather that's in it, eh?' Then she saw his arm and exclaimed, 'Dear to goodness, Trapper, what's come over your arm?'

She was a tall stringy woman with big hands and big

feet, and dressed as she was with a man's boots on her big feet and a big waterproof cape covering her from the rain that plastered her grey hair to her face, she was not a bonny sight. However, her concern for Alasdair was kindly enough and he would have made her a civil reply if Torquil had not come up with a load of turnips just at that moment.

Alasdair knew all about Torquil and his animals. Roaming the hill the way he did on his trapping rounds there was not much that missed him and many a time he had seen Torquil crouched quiet beside a nest or lair, or working away at cleaning his cages in the burn beside Morag's house with Dondo perching on his head or Polar lying across his shoulder. The sight of the boy now, and him so friendly with Morag, brought back all his anger against her.

'Never mind my arm,' he said sourly. 'It's yourself you should be worrying about before that witch, Morag MacLeod, puts the evil eye on you and your house.'

The driver of the Land Rover straightened up at this with his mouth open in alarm and Torquil threw down his load of turnips, his face flaming scarlet.

'I'll punch your head if you speak like that of Mistress MacLeod!' he shouted.

He doubled up his fists and glowered at Alasdair but the Woman caught him by the shoulder and swung him round to face her.

'What do *you* know of the cailleach?' she demanded. 'Did I not order you not to go near her house?'

'He was not heeding you,' Alasdair put in maliciously

before Torquil could answer. 'He is as thick as thieves with her. They're two of a kind, they are, talking away to ferrets and rabbits and birds and such-like as if they were Christian creatures like ourselves!'

Even the Woman's bony grasp on his shoulder could not stop Torquil now. Beside himself with rage he shouted, 'I would rather be her kind than your kind, Trapper, for she has a heart and you have none!'

This time it was the Woman who cut in on Alasdair before he could reply. 'What are you talking about, Trapper?' she demanded. 'What has Torquil been up to?'

'Be quiet, you!' Torquil commanded Alasdair fiercely. 'I will tell her myself.'

He put the Woman's hand from his shoulder so that he could stand upright and speak with dignity, for though he had disobeyed her he was not ashamed of what he had done. She listened to him speaking and said never a word until he had finished telling her how Morag had given his animals a refuge. But when he told her that he had seen the kelpie too and began to defend Morag against all the things that were said about her, she interrupted him.

'The old woman has addled your wits with her spells and charms,' she said firmly. 'I will get the minister to say a prayer over you and put all this heathen nonsense out of your head.'

'You will need to put more than one prayer between you and the witch,' Alasdair said. 'This storm is of her doing too – she told me so herself not an hour ago. She said that she had raised it with a spell and that it would last for three days.'

'Lord save us!' cried the Woman, and 'Liar!' cried Torquil, both in the one breath, and 'Into the house with you,' the Woman commanded Torquil before he could say anything else. 'I'll deal with you as soon as I get this load of turnips away. Into the house!'

She turned to the driver who had been standing like a man struck dumb while all this was going on and began to give him orders about his load, and Torquil went slowly towards the house. Behind him he heard the voices of the other three raised in argument, with Alasdair's voice getting louder and louder until it beat down the sound of the other two.

'I will settle the question, you'll see!' he was bawling. 'As soon as this storm is over I am going back up the hill and I'll blow the kelpie's pool sky-high – with dynamite!'

Ten minutes later, Torquil heard the sound of the Land Rover driving off and then the squelching of the Woman's big boots as she came up the muddy path to the back door. She came in and looked at him in silence and Torquil looked at her.

'I couldn't kill them,' he said at last. 'You cannot kill anything you love. It would be murder.'

'You disobeyed me because of them,' the Woman said grimly. 'You went to that old woman's house after I warned you to stay away from her. So to the sin of disobedience you have added the sin of pride, thinking you knew better than me what was good for you.'

'Punish me then!' cried Torquil, 'but don't touch the animals, please! They've done no harm.'

'That is for me to decide,' the Woman said angrily. 'And as for you, you will not stir out of this house while the storm is on, do you hear? When the weather has cleared I will go up the hill myself and find out what is behind all this business. And if you disobey me this time, you will be thrashed. Do you understand?'

Torquil nodded miserably. He understood all right but he also knew that he would have to risk that thrashing after what Alasdair had said about blowing up the kelpie's pool. It would break Morag's heart to have such a thing happen and how could he let it without making some attempt to warn her? As for his animals, he thought, he would have to make some plan to rescue them before the Woman could get her hands on them. Perhaps the Naturalist would let him keep them at Kiltarlity.

Maybe the Woman suspected what he was thinking. Anyhow, she took no chances but all that day while the storm still raged outside she kept him locked in the house and at night she came to his room two or three times to make sure he was still there. The next day was the same but that night, what with having lost her sleep the night before, she slept heavily. Torquil lay and listened to her snoring until he was sure she would not wake up, then quietly he got up and dressed, put back the bolt on his window, opened it and slid out on to the sill.

The storm caught him up at once like a giant's

hands, but he steadied himself against the wall of the house till he had recovered his breath; then with his head down against the rain and the wind he set off up the hill. Morag's house was in darkness of course when

he reached there, but he bent down to the keyhole and whistled through it as loud as he could and a few minutes later she came to the door calling, 'Who's there?'

'It's me, Torquil!' he called through the keyhole and she opened the door.

Minutes later, Morag had made up the fire in the

kitchen and Torquil was drinking hot milk and telling her what the Woman and Alasdair had threatened to do.

'The Naturalist will let me keep my animals with him,' he finished. 'But what about Alasdair? You'll have to stop him, Mistress Morag.'

'I know,' said Morag. 'I know. But what can I do? He is a big strong man, and look at me. I am old and weak. What *can* I do?'

'Oh, he is wicked, wicked!' cried Torquil. 'He is telling lies about you too, saying that you told him you raised this storm with a spell!'

'That's no lie,' Morag said, 'I *did* raise the storm. Do you not remember I told you I had a plan to drive all these people away from my house?'

The cup went clattering from Torquil's hand. He rose slowly to his feet staring at Morag. 'Was that your plan?' he whispered. '*Witchcraft!*'

Morag looked at his white face and staring eyes and all at once she realized how wrong she had been not to trust him. Without a word she rose and took the key of her grandmother's little old black cupboard off its hook, unlocked the cupboard and took out the book of magic.

'Sit down, Torquil,' she said, 'and listen to me. I am going to read you from this book that belonged to Elizabeth MacLeod who was my grandmother and a white witch. It is all in the Gaelic or you could read it for yourself.'

'How do I know you will read truly then?' Torquil whispered.

'Give me your cross of rowan,' said Morag.

Torquil drew the little cross of rowan wood from his pocket and laid it on the table between them. Morag put the tips of her fingers on it and said solemnly,

'I swear by the sacred wood of the tree that bred the tree from which this cross was made that I will read truly what is written in the book of Elizabeth Mac-Leod.'

Then she opened the book of magic and read the spell for raising a storm. And at the end of reading the spell she read also,

And I, Elizabeth MacLeod, being a white witch who has harmed no one with her power, do conjure any who read this book not to cast this spell for destruction and malice, but only for the protection of the weak. And if they do as I command, the storm will pass over and above them and they will receive no harm from it. But whoso casts this spell in malice, my curse shall fall on them and they will be destroyed in the storm that shall arise from the spell.

Morag closed the book. 'All this have I done, Torquil,' she said. 'Now you shall be the judge if I have acted from malice or for the protection of the weak.' She rose to her feet and went to the front door. 'Come,' she said to Torquil. 'Come with me out into the storm. If you believe that the spell raised the storm then you must believe also that the storm will destroy me who raised it, if I did so from malice.'

Torquil put the rowan cross back in his pocket and rose to his feet. Morag opened the front door and he followed her as she stepped outside. At once he was caught up and whipped and tossed like a cork in the torrents of rain and wind, and with a cry of terror he thrust his hands blindly out for support. His hands were caught and held in Morag's own. He looked up and saw her standing calm and still in the centre of the storm, her hair not so much as ruffled, her face turned up to the sky so peaceful that she might have been looking up to the blue, windless sky of a summer day.

Torquil saw all this in the light that streamed from the open doorway, and maybe it was only the light of the lamp there but he could have sworn in that moment that the light came from Morag herself, and it seemed to him that it was the reflection of some great goodness that shone out of her and that no storm or night could darken.

The feeling moved him to step closer to her, and as soon as he did this he felt the wind stop tearing at him and the rain streamed past him without touching him, and it was as if he stood in a warm lit room with the storm outside its walls and himself safe from all harm.

Morag looked down at him. 'I used a witch's spell,' she said. 'Am I a witch then, Torquil?'

'No, Mistress Morag, you are a good woman,' Torquil said, yet even as he spoke he understood the trouble that would fall on her because of the storm and that he could do nothing to save her from it. He clenched her hands in his and at the touch of her thin old fingers between his strong young ones a great sorrow for Morag gripped him. 'I am sorry for you, Mistress Morag,' he said, and though it puzzled her to hear him talk like this he would not tell her why he had said it.

'Let her have one more day of peace,' he thought to himself, and to Morag he said, 'You are not to worry about me or my animals when the storm is finished. We shall be safe with the Naturalist.'

'Then there is only Alasdair to worry about,' said Morag, greatly relieved. 'I will ask the kelpie what to do about him. It is his pool after all, and surely he will think of something.'

This was a thought that had not occurred to Torquil, but as soon as Morag mentioned it he saw right away that it was the only thing to do. But he took his leave of her with a heavy heart all the same, and when he had slipped back into bed that night he lay awake for a long time thinking of her and wondering if the Trapper had got the dynamite to blow up the kelpie's pool.

CHAPTER 8

The Land of Heart's Desire

Now you cannot just go into a shop and buy dynamite like you would buy a bar of soap or a pound of beef! You must have a licence and permission from the police and so on, but this sort of thing did not bother the Trapper who had not much respect for the law at the best of times. One of his friends was a rough sort of fellow that worked at a gravel quarry quite near Inverness, and to him Alasdair went as soon as he had seen a doctor about his arm.

A bit of money changed hands, heads were put together, and a deal of whispering took place. By the next morning the explosives store at the quarry was lighter by a number of sticks of dynamite, Alasdair had them stowed safely away in the bothy where he kept his tools, and then he was free to go into Inverness and idle away his time till the end of the storm.

In the town he bought a newspaper and read all about the havoc the storm (which was now in its second day) was causing. Trees had been blown down, said the paper, rivers were in flood, and there had even been a landslide that had blocked the railway line to the south and held up a train with a lot of great and important London people aboard. Curiously enough, no one had been hurt by all these things, but Alasdair didn't notice that. He was too busy brooding on the fact that it was the storm which had caused his dam to break before he could get the pearls. His arm was still throbbing badly and this, of course, did not improve his temper one little bit. All morning he brooded, and by the afternoon his spite at Morag had got the better of his common sense.

'I'll see the old witch gets what she deserves,' he muttered to himself. He put the newspaper in his pocket and went along to the hotel where there were a lot of newspaper men staying.

'I'll tell you who you can blame for this storm,' he said to one of the reporters. 'I know who caused it. It was Morag MacLeod, the witch-woman. She raised it with a spell to get rid of all you fellows.'

Well, naturally the reporter just laughed at this for superstitious nonsense, which sent Alasdair off in a rage fit to choke him. Back he went to the bothy where he had hidden the dynamite and began to pack it into his game-bag all ready to take up the hill as soon as the storm stopped. And there he waited for the next thirty-six hours, clutching his wounded arm and brooding over his wrongs till he had nursed his rage into the grandfather and grandmother of all tempers!

As it happened, however, the very unreasonableness of his display of rage had made the reporter think there might be something in what the Trapper had told him. He thought about it for a while after Alasdair had banged out of the hotel, and the more he thought the more his curiosity grew until he decided to talk it over with someone.

'But not a Highlander,' he thought – which was perfectly natural, he being a Lowlander himself. 'They're all far too superstitious!'

He walked into the hotel lounge and who should he see there but the professor of the scientific expedition sitting in a corner with a gloomy expression on his face. This was the sort of person he was looking for! He went over and sat down beside him, and like everybody else in the town was doing they began to talk about the storm. Very soon the reporter was repeating what Alasdair had said to him, but greatly to his surprise the professor didn't laugh at it. Instead, he looked gloomier than ever and said,

'They are a strange people, the Highlanders. He might well be telling the truth for all we know.'

'But do you believe this old woman is a witch, sir?' asked the reporter.

'I can tell you,' said the professor, 'that when I stepped out of my tent yesterday morning I saw a dam all spattered with blood across the burn where no dam had been the night before. And when I spoke to the old woman she warned me that a storm would come within the hour. I don't know what connection the two things had, if any, for I never found out yet who built the dam. But I did see the storm break. It came out of a clear blue sky and it soaked me, *but the rain and the wind did not touch the old woman!* Maybe you can find a natural explanation for that, but I cannot.'

And that was that. The reporter had got his story about Morag, and one moreover that was confirmed by no less a person than the scientific professor, and he lost no time in getting it published in the evening edition of his newspaper. By the morning of the third day of the storm the buzz about Morag had risen to a roar, for there was not a newspaper in the land that did not have headlines about the witch of Abriachan.

People poured into Inverness from all directions by train, bus and car (air traffic having been grounded because of the storm) – and there was not a room in a hotel or boarding-house to be had for love or money. The shops were sold out of wellington boots and mackintoshes. The Town Council had an emergency meeting to pass a bye-law forbidding the practice of witchcraft within the county of Inverness, and the children of the town invented a new game called, *'Run, witchy, run!'*

All the campers and picnickers and hikers had been driven off the hill by the end of the second day of the storm, and the excitement in the town grew as they told how they had seen Morag going about her work on the croft as unconcerned as if the storm didn't exist.

'And no more it did for her,' said some of them, 'for we passed close by her and we could see her clothes were dry as a bone and there was not even a drop of rain shining in her hair.'

'Three days she said it would last,' they reminded one another, and everyone made up their minds that when the storm came to an end after the third day they would go up the hill and have a good look at the witch of Abriachan.

Now you may say that Morag was an old fool not to have realized the stir her spell would make once people knew about it, but Morag was far from being a fool. The truth was that she had never learned to think like people who live in cities and she just did not realize (as Torquil had done) how different her way of thinking was to theirs. She did not think the idea of using a spell at all strange and because of this she never gave a thought to what people might be thinking or saying about her and the storm, and it certainly did not cross her mind that the spell would make matters worse rather than better for her, in the end.

The only thing that worried her was Alasdair's threat to blow up the kelpie's pool with dynamite and on the second night of the storm she went down to the pool as soon as Torquil had left her, determined to call the kelpie till he came so that she could warn him of his danger. This was the first time she had used her power over him – the power he had told her was a witch's power – but she excused herself by saying that it was for his own good and he would be grateful to her when he knew.

She waited by the edge of the pool, calling and calling, and when at last the kelpie came she told him what Alasdair meant to do and how the dynamite would blow the bed of the burn sky-high and destroy his pool.

'There is only one day left to decide what to do,'

she told him. 'Alasdair is certain to be back the day after tomorrow when the storm finishes.'

The kelpie looked at Morag and noticed that her clothes were quite dry in spite of the rain that was lashing down.

'This is a strange storm,' he remarked, 'and it is strange you should be so sure it has still a day to run before it comes to an end.'

'Och, I am getting tired of explaining this,' said Morag. 'I know about the storm because I raised it myself with a spell from my grandmother's book of magic to drive all these people off the hill.'

'Then you are in greater trouble than I am,' said the kelpie.

'I am not in any trouble now!' cried Morag. 'The strangers have all left the hill and I am back to my old peaceful ways.'

'They will come back,' the kelpie told her. 'More and more of them will come back.'

Morag stared at him, not understanding what he meant, and the kelpie looked back at her with a great sadness in his old face.

'Mistress Morag,' he said, 'you have had a place in the human world for seventy-three years because you were like them, and so you were one of them. But now you have lost that place in your world because you have done something that will cause you to be called a witch, and they have no place any more for witches in their world. And so you can never again be an ordinary old woman living by her lone and contented in a little house on the hill-side. You will be a sight to see, a joke to laugh at, or a story to tell. And in all the world there will never more be peace or pity for you.'

And Morag, who was not so stupid that she could not understand the world's way of thinking when it was explained to her, whispered,

'What am I to do?'

'Will you trust me?' asked the kelpie.

'Why should I not trust you,' she said sadly. 'You are my only friend now.'

'There is a land,' said the kelpie, 'a land of heart's desire where I could take you and none could follow. It is far away and it has many names, but in the Gaelic it is called *Tir-nan-Og* and it is the land of eternal youth.'

'I am not young,' whispered Morag.

'You will be young there,' the kelpie said. 'All the beautiful women and great heroes of olden times live there, and they are for ever young.'

Morag wrung her hands in distress. 'I am not brave or beautiful,' she cried.

'Your heart is good,' said the kelpie. 'A good heart will show a brave and beautiful face in Tir-nan-Og.'

'But my little house,' Morag wept. 'How could I leave my little house I love so well, where I have lived so long?'

'Home is in your heart,' said the kelpie. 'Your little house will be there for you in Tir-nan-Og if you carry the memory of it there in your heart.'

'Give me but one day then to put all in order,' Morag pleaded. 'Then I will come with you.'

'Only one day then,' said the kelpie, 'or it will be too late and nothing I can do will save you from the reckoning.'

He disappeared into the pool and Morag went slowly back to her house, thinking of all he had said.

She was up with the dawn the next day and for the last time she milked the cow and collected the eggs from her white hens. For the last time she swept and dusted and polished, cleaned the windows and weeded the garden and fed Torquil's animals. When she had finished that evening she put on her best dress, a clean white cap and apron, and her string of pearls and sat down at the table in the kitchen with pen and ink and a sheet of paper in front of her.

She dipped the pen in the ink and wrote a letter to Torquil, but she did not address it to him for fear that if it was read by anyone else his name would be linked with hers and bring more unhappiness to him. Instead, she went out to the shed and hid it in the straw of Polar's cage where no one else was likely to look but himself.

Then she went back to the house and looked all round her. There was not a pin out of place or a speck of dust to be seen and she loved her little house so much that she felt her heart would break to leave it. The kelpie was right, she knew, about what would happen, and she believed she would find Tir-nan-Og as he had described it to her. But still the time of parting lay heavy on her and the ache of it was bitter in her heart.

'I will leave the door open,' she said aloud, 'so that I can walk straight in at the open door of my house when I reach Tir-nan-Og.'

She went outside leaving the door open behind her and the polished knob of the door-latch winked good-bye to her. Then she went down to the pool to find the kelpie.

He was waiting there for her beside the pool – a great, strong, black horse with shoulders like polished ebony and the water still streaming from his tail and mane. Morag stood and looked at him for a long moment. The great horse looked at her, and it never moved.

'*Will you trust me?*' he had asked her the evening before, and she had trusted him then. She trusted him now, and so she walked towards him. She grasped his mane, and still the black horse never moved. She stood on a stone beside him, swung herself on to his back, and the black horse moved.

Morag closed her eyes and held her breath. Now was the kelpie's chance. Now, if he wanted to drown her, all he had to do was to plunge into his pool and carry her down with him to his home at the bottom of the water.

The black horse moved towards the pool. She felt the gathering together of the great limbs, the bunching of the powerful muscles. Then the kelpie leapt, and with one soaring bound it was over the pool and galloping westwards across the hill in great leaping strides. Morag opened her eyes and looked straight ahead as she rode, and though the tears of parting ran down her cheeks like rain she did not once look back at her little house, for the memory of it was so clearly imprinted on her heart that she knew she was sure to see it again, exactly as she had left it, when she reached Tir-nan-Og.

No mortal ear could have heard the kelpie passing through the night for the great black hooves of it were soundless in their stride as feathers falling. But two people were awake to see it bearing Morag away, and these two were Torquil and the Woman.

In the croft at the foot of the hill, Torquil sat sleepless on the edge of his bed. The door of his room opened quietly and the Woman's head peered round it. She saw him sitting there and came quickly in, the lighted candle in her hand making her shadow leap up big and dark on the wall behind her.

'Get to bed, boy!' she said sharply.

'I cannot sleep,' he said, and the sadness in his voice shamed her for she knew well it was concern for Morag that was troubling him.

'It is the storm that is making you feel restless,' she said more kindly.

She put down her candle-stick and went to the window, but as her hand went up to draw the curtains against the storm she gave a great cry that brought Torquil running to her side.

'Look there!' she cried. 'Do you see her? It is Morag MacLeod the old witch-woman riding by on a great black horse!'

Torquil peered through the glass and then he said

something that caused the Woman to draw back sharply and stare at him.

'You must have a fever, boy,' she said.

'I have no fever,' Torquil replied, and he told the Woman again what he had seen.

The Woman touched her hand to his brow and when she felt it was quite cool she backed away from him with a frightened look on her face. 'No, you have no fever, your brow is cool,' she muttered. She picked up her candle-stick. '*You are bewitched!*' she cried.

She fled from the room and the sound of her voice wailing '*Bewitched! Bewitched!*' came echoing back to Torquil as he sat on alone in the dark with the vision of what he had seen in his mind, and the storm crying to him from outside the window.

CHAPTER 9

The Witch of Abriachan

THE first people to reach Morag's house after she left it were two tall policemen who had been sent up from Inverness to investigate all the strange things that were said to be going on at Abriachan.

They arrived at dawn the next morning, left their motor-cycles at the edge of the hill-road and took off their oilskin capes – for the storm had stopped exactly as it had been said in the spell, at dawn on the fourth morning after it was cast. They tramped across the heather in the bright morning sunshine to Morag's house and found the door standing wide open and the house deserted.

'She'll turn up. She wouldn't go away and leave everything just like that,' said the one who was the sergeant.

They waited for a while to see if she would come, but when an hour had passed and there was still no sign of her the sergeant went back to Inverness and left the constable on guard at the house.

Torquil saw the policeman standing at the front door as he came running across the hill-side a little later on that morning. The sergeant had already passed him going down the road on his motor-cycle and he

117

ran up to the house with his heart full of fear for what he might find there.

'Where is Mistress MacLeod? Have you seen her?' he cried out to the constable.

'Neither hide nor hair of her,' the man said. 'The door was open when we came and she might be at the foot of Loch Ness for all we know.'

Torquil thought of what he had seen in the hours of darkness and his heart went right down into his boots. To give himself time to think he said,

'I'll feed my animals then. They're in the shed at the back.'

'Oh, they're yours, are they?' said the policeman. 'Man, that's a proper zoo you have there!'

Torquil hardly heard him he was so busy thinking of the meaning of what he had seen. He went into the shed and straight to Polar's cage for he could always think better with Polar curled round his neck. As soon as he touched the straw he felt Morag's note. He drew it out and went to the door of the shed to read it. There were only a few lines in it.

I understand now the sorrow that was in your heart for me, and so I am going with the kelpie to a far-off land where none may follow. This is to take my leave of you and to tell you that if you use wisely the great gift you have, neither this sorrow nor any other will walk at your side for long. Do not grieve for me then, for the place I go to now is the land of heart's desire, and there I shall be young and happy and at peace for ever.

Torquil folded the note and for a long time he stood

at the door of the shed looking at the bright morning outside. Every leaf and blade on the hill-side glistened with the jewels of rain the storm had scattered. Larks sprang singing from the heather into the eye of the sun and in the kelpie's pool the little burn-trout leaping at the morning hatch of flies were like silver darts flicking in and out of the golden-brown water. But Torquil saw and heard nothing of it all for his mind was black and blind with grief for the passing of Morag and for the death of his dream-world.

There was one ray of comfort for him. At least now he knew what had happened to her and he understood the meaning of the strange thing he had seen in the hours of darkness. And he knew now, also, that he was not bewitched as the Woman had said. His sight had been clearer than hers, that was all, clear enough – as Morag's letter proved – to have seen her as she really was when she vanished with the kelpie.

It was the thought of the Woman that drove him on now and shook him from the grip of his grief. There was no time to be lost if he was to save his animals and so he bolted the shed door and set off at a run for the Naturalist's house at Kiltarlity. As he ran he made up his mind that where his animals went this time, he would go, and by the time he arrived everything was sorted out in his mind. He poured the whole story out without stopping to draw breath.

'I can take up the training you spoke about now, sir,' he finished. 'She'll not want to have me at the croft now. She'd be afraid to have me in the house and her thinking Mistress MacLeod has bewitched me.'

'We'll see,' the Naturalist said. 'If she doesn't want you it's the way out we've been looking for.'

That was all he said for he was far too wise a man to question Torquil about his story. The way he looked at it, Torquil might well be talking a lot of nonsense about Morag, but even if it was nonsense – well, at least he was an honest boy and would be honestly mistaken in what he said. He hustled him into his jeep and the pair of them bumped off back up the hill and down the other side to the Woman's croft, and there things turned out just as Torquil had said they would.

'Take him and welcome,' she told the Naturalist. 'He is my own brother's sister-in-law's son, but kin of mine though he is I'll not have a boy with the evil eye on him in *my* house a day longer than I can help.'

'Evil fiddlesticks!' the Naturalist snorted into his beard. 'Come on, Torquil, we'll get your animals now.'

And up the hill they went again to Morag's house. The policeman there was having a terrible job keeping the sightseers away and answering all their questions, but the Naturalist was such a well-known and respected man that he made no objections to him shifting the animals out of the shed. He watched the jeep with Torquil and the Naturalist and all the animals in it rattling off and thought it was one problem solved anyway, and he wondered what he should do if Morag herself did not appear by the end of the day.

By nightfall when there was still no sign of her and all the curious crowds had gone, he decided there was nothing for it but to lock the door of the house and go back to the police station at Inverness to report.

'Something must have happened to her,' they decided there, and soon they had search parties out all over the hill with sticks and torches and walkie-talkie sets. They saw no sign of Morag of course, but they did find someone. And that someone was Alasdair the Trapper lying unconscious at the side of the burn.

As usual, Alasdair had only himself to blame for his misfortunes. He had come up the hill on the heels of the two policemen that morning and waited all day beside the burn till the second of them had left Morag's house. Then he had opened up his game-bag and taken out the dynamite, and just as he had threatened to do he had blown the kelpie's pool sky-high.

The noise of the explosion echoed all over the hillside rousing people from their beds and bringing them running across the hill to Morag's house. And the first man who got there swore that a great black horse had passed him on the road, running like the wind.

'He was the biggest horse that ever I saw in my life,' said the man, 'and a skin on him as black as the inside of a chimney.'

'There's no horse like that hereabouts,' said the other men.

'Nor ever will be,' said the first man, 'for big as he was and fast as he ran his hooves never made a sound on the road. And no natural horse that was ever foaled can run without a sound!'

He looked round at all the other men. '*It was the kelpie I saw,*' he said.

No one said yes and no one said no to this. They looked down at Alasdair lying all wet and battered and bruised among the scattered rocks and mud of the burn, and they saw that the great ugly bruise on his forehead was the exact shape of the hoof of a horse.

Just then, one of the police search parties came across the hill and when they found what had happened they took Alasdair back to Inverness with them. The crofters were left shaking their heads over the whole business and wondering what on earth it was all about till one of them spied something white gleaming in the mud. He picked it up.

'Look!' said he. 'A pearl!'

Everyone crowded round to look. Then they looked at one another and the same thought was in all their minds. '*Where there's one pearl there may be more!*' But none of them wanted his neighbour to know what he was thinking and so they all said good night and scattered to their homes.

The next day you might have seen people poking around in the grass and the mud where Alasdair had blown up the burn, but none of them said what he was looking for and none of them found any pearls. The only unusual thing to be seen was a set of horse's hoof-prints and these, it was noticed, did not lead down to the burn as they would have done if they had been made by a horse going there to drink. Instead, they pointed outwards – *from the bed of the burn towards the bank!*

As was only to be expected this put a certain fear into the crofters. The search for the pearls was quickly given up once the hoof-prints were noticed. No one dared to go back again to look for them and so a proper search has never been made, and for all anyone knows, they may still be lying there scattered among the mud and stones thrown up by the explosion.

As for Alasdair the Trapper, he got three months in jail for the unlawful use of explosives! The bruise on his forehead faded in time but it has never quite vanished, and any crofter who meets him on the hill-side nowadays 'makes horns' in his direction for fear of the mark shaped like a horse's hoof that he carries on the middle of his forehead.

Alasdair is a sadder and a wiser man now. Never again has he been heard to call himself a modern man that does not believe such nonsense as kelpies, and he would not thank you for a million pearls supposing they were to be set and strung by the finest jeweller in the land.

And Morag herself? The police search parties never found her, of course, though they searched every inch of the hill-side for days after she disappeared. They questioned everybody who lived at Abriachan as well, but they could not find anyone, apart from Torquil and the Woman, who had seen her on the night she disappeared.

A sergeant and an inspector came to the Woman's house one day and the inspector asked questions while the sergeant wrote down the answers.

'Tell us exactly what you saw that night,' the inspector began.

'I saw Morag MacLeod riding by my house on a great black horse,' the Woman told him.

'Which direction was she headed in?' he asked and she said, 'West.'

'And did anyone else in the house see her?' the inspector went on.

'Aye, the boy Torquil MacVinish that's living with the Naturalist over Kiltarlity way now, but you'll not get much sense out of him,' the Woman said sourly.

'There's nothing else you can think of to give us a clue, is there?' the inspector asked. 'Anything strange about her appearance, for instance?'

The Woman wasn't at all keen to answer this question but the inspector pressed her and at last she said, 'Well, there was a strange thing. I could see her clear, you understand, because she passed close to the house and – well, she was weeping!' And then, because she was kind enough under her rough manner, the Woman added, 'I've felt sorry for the old woman since when I thought about it, for she was weeping sore, poor soul, as if she had a great sorrow to bear.'

Well, the sergeant wrote all this down. Then he and the inspector went over to Kiltarlity and the inspector told Torquil what the Woman had said and asked him did he see Morag too and where was she going and so on. Torquil looked at the Naturalist standing listening to all this and he said,

'They'll never believe me if I tell them what I saw.'

'That's neither here nor there,' the Naturalist said. 'Tell the truth, boy, and shame the devil.'

And so Torquil turned to the inspector and he said, 'I saw Mistress MacLeod ride by on a black horse that night, and true enough it was west she was going. But she was not an old woman when I saw her, and she was not weeping. She was young again, just like she was when she had her picture painted in a white dress with her long gold hair hanging down her back, and she was looking towards a great light that shone out of the west and I could see that her face was glad and shining as she rode towards it.'

The policemen looked at one another over Torquil's head, smiling a little. The sergeant closed his notebook without writing down a word and when they got out-side again he said to the inspector,

'Can you beat that for a story?'

'Aye, he has a wild imagination, sure enough,' agreed the inspector, and that was the end of it so far as they were concerned.

There were one or two stories in the newspapers after that about the mystery of Morag's disappearance but when nothing further happened they soon found other things to write about. But on the hill, the argu-ment still raged.

She was a witch that was in league with the kelpie, said some, and some said that she was just a poor old woman that had been carried off by the kelpie. 'How could she be a witch,' they asked, 'when she was weeping as she rode?'

This was quite a point of course, for it is quite true that witches cannot weep, and so it has never been proved to this day whether or not Morag MacLeod, the Witch of Abriachan, really was a witch.

The story that Torquil had told the policemen became known after a time, of course, but it was all put down to his imagination. Indeed, there were times in his new life with the Naturalist when the memory of his time with Morag grew so faint that Torquil himself thought he must have imagined it all. When he thought like that, however, he had only to touch his little cross of rowan wood to step back through the secret door of the dream-world where he could smell the sharp, sweet scent of white roses, taste royal crowdie on his tongue again, and feel the spell of stories told by a bright fire on a winter's evening.

But it was only for a moment that he could ever recapture this feeling, and this was just as well for Torquil, for a moment of longing for a world that has vanished is as much as anyone can bear.

As time went by, then, everybody found their own explanation for the events on the hill that summer, and it was only when they remembered the pearl that had been found the night the Trapper dynamited the kelpie's pool that they realized there were pieces missing from the puzzle and wondered what was the true explanation that lay behind it all.

Well, they will know now if they read this, and anyone who cares can go up the hill to Abriachan and see Morag's house still standing there. The burn no longer flows past it for Alasdair's dynamiting changed its course, and the house itself is breaking down as houses do that are not lived in. But the walls of clay and straw are still strong and so is the roof of pine-boughs and heather.

And far below the house you can still see Loch Ness glinting in the valley as Morag used to see it every day before she rode off with the kelpie, and as maybe she still sees it, blue and shining in Tir-nan-Og.